IF I CLOSE MY EYES

ΣΆΡΚΑ

First edition, 2023

ISBN 979-8-9879849-0-1

SARKA Publishing LLC
sarkapublishing.com
@sarka.publishing

Cover image by Forsyth Harmon
Designed by Ben Pease

IF I CLOSE MY EYES

BEN FAMA

Shooting Stars!

Model, actress and doll Marsy-Rose Arenas posted a selfie with fellow shooting victim Jesse Shore on Tuesday at a taco truck near Echo Park. Arenas, who is engaged to *Retinue* star Marc Pevier, still has her ring on, according to sources near her.

The playdate lasted into the night, where the two were seen partying with an unknown friend in Chinatown. Photos show 19-year-old Shore snorting what appears to be cocaine in a Miata convertible with an unknown female friend. Another photo showed him wiping a white substance from his jacket collar.

Both Arenas and Shore were treated for wounds after a fanatical shooter opened fire at Kim Kardashian's book signing in midtown Manhattan last month. A network crew member was killed in the incident. Kris Jenner, matriarch and self-purported queen of the Kardashian empire, told reporters the incident was "tragic" in a press conference last week.

Arenas' agent declined to comment on the status of her engagement to Pevier, or whether she was having an affair with Shore after their meet-cute. Shore is the son of the late screenwriter Patricia Shore, who won an Emmy nomination for her miniseries *Until I See Palm Trees Again.*

Chapter 1: Closed Set

Jesse Shore was watching reality television on his phone. It was his birthday, the solstice, a hot but tender June day, and when he'd gotten the email—his Uncle Lee had jokingly entered him into a lottery—he'd dashed from his job at Atelier, tape measure still around his neck, and caught a cab uptown to collect his prize: the small but heavy photo book, signed by Kim Kardashian herself, at an in-store meet-and-greet. A line trailed down 555 Fifth Avenue beneath the franchise's dependable and saddening gray-algae color branding. Tuning out the girls taking selfies, the teenager with a speaker blasting from in his backpack, he envied the characters in this scene as he squinted into the small screen at the couple who bantered and flirted in the air-conditioned living room of their Calabasas home. Kourtney, the sexy and levelheaded older sister of the large family, had strapped a dildo over her clothes, preening (for the cameras, not her boyfriend, surely) and leaping about. The prosthetic, a lengthy, censored purple smudge, sprang languidly from her waist toward her boyfriend's face as he sat distracted by his texts. In this episode, he'd been urging her to try anal with him. She'd planned a stunt—nudged by producers, no doubt—and some lucky PA must have helped her into the kinky gear. *Irony, contingency, solidarity*, Jesse thought to himself. *I could have been born this asshole, instead of myself.*

Jesse fell easily for the allure of this type of celebrity: the reality TV star who didn't need to fully articulate herself. The genre was full of half-enunciated characters, drawn up in the cutting room, supplemented by A-list cameos, tabloid fantasias, defamatory gossip sites, endorsements, modeling contracts, spin-off products.

The stars of reality television were always already cultural ruins. And despite what is commonly the situation and story of these shows, the family drama was a red herring: the conflict is the desire for more screen time against the fickle antagonism of the viewership, the passing time that ebbs and flows the ratings toward and away from high-res horizons.

A call from his father broke his focus. He denied it before he even considered answering. Thoughts of his father set off a daisy chain of bad feelings—the guilt of being an absent son; years of bad behavior. He was turning nineteen and the thought of carrying these feelings into his twenties rested heavily. He began a bleak, brief meditation, closing his eyes to reset his composure. He shouldn't be here, he knew. He felt embarrassed when Uncle Lee asked if he had his birthday off; poor planning and a patchy work record meant working on his birthday. He was a mess; this wasn't the life he'd imagined for himself when he'd moved here less than a year ago. He felt himself becoming emotional, a familiar knotty block built in his throat, and he considered leaving, though the triumph and shared joy of sending a photo of his prize to Uncle Lee kept him waiting.

The sun seemed bigger today, hissing down. He longed to be in the shade, near water or standing in a pool. His discomfort pivoted to anxiety as he counted bodies from the door back to where he waited; there were hundreds ahead as the line wound through the store. A squad of policemen confined bodies to the sidewalk. The possibility he would go back to work empty-handed disappointed him, and he wanted to see what a net worth of 85 million dollars looked like in person. People began skipping the line, trying to enter the store. Anti-fur advocates disguised as fans were shouting at Kim. One of them had set fire to a cardboard display. The scene on his phone still played. A family argument wailed through his earbuds. He yanked them out.

The store was evacuated, disorder ruled; Jesse watched the sidewalk swell with an assemblage of panicked customers as the camera crew captured the melee. Jesse became frightened, but there she was, her majesty, hunching in large-frame Saint Laurent sunglasses towards a black Escalade, hooding her head and face with her blazer. Jesse took photographs alongside a rush of hopeful fanatics, pushing against the volume of people still trying to escape the store. The protestors jostled themselves in front of the cameras. *Are my kids on your back? Fifty dead animals for one fur coat.* A shift in the compact crowd rocked Jesse. He lost his footing, stumbling under the mass, taking a few people down with him, losing his grip on his phone. As he scanned for it, he locked eyes with another of the fallen, a younger teenage boy wearing army boots, his face frozen in pain. Jesse became fearful again when he realized the boy had a knee against his neck and was being arrested.

A temporary clearing formed and anonymous hands found his own, hoisting him back into the storm surge of bodies. People were yelling for Kim's attention, her handlers and overwhelmed security staff beginning to panic. Someone lit a string of fireworks. A boom mic went down, a mast collapsed by the mutinous.

Jesse thought he'd caught sight of his phone among the riot. But as the pops continued (they almost sounded cute, like snapping bubble wrap), a round struck him in the belly. He felt the pinch, and saw the blood. His vision spotted out as violent shivers of cold overtook him. He felt concrete and heard a woman screaming, *oh my god, oh my god*, then woke up in Mount Sinai, hours after his birthday had ended.

The incident was immediately reported worldwide: a group of teens temporarily living in Tompkins Square Park planned the protest and claimed no affiliation to the shooting. The shooter was an unstable 30-something celebrity fanatic who'd driven up from a Maryland suburb. Files on his computer combined with online writing exposed him to be a celebrity stalker and men's rights advocate. Security at the store had been put on alert years ago after he'd bitten another celebrity author, an incident that was reported on in *Page Six* and the *New York Daily News*. After he was taken alive at the site of the public shooting, his attorneys claimed the violent protestors had agitated him into a psychotic state; he believed he was protecting Kim.

A member of the network's camera crew had been shot in the spine and died in surgery. Another female was struck in the shoulder and expected to fully recover. The Kardashians denounced the incident in a heartfelt tribute video.

Lucky Jesse: the bullet that struck his abdomen passed through him without hitting his major organs. Lying in the recovery room in the days that followed, in near-sleep paralysis due to the morphine, he dreamed he'd made a dying wish to executive producer and show creator Ryan Seacrest for a cameo on *Keeping Up with the Kardashians*, pleading that without a heaven or hell to cradle his soul, he wished on earth for the things he must. This vision ended with Kim herself standing over him pointing a smoking handgun as Jesse lay dying on the wide brick steps of a

Calabasas mansion.

Jesse, first to his horror, then delight, saw the uncanny bustle of a reality crew preparing to film when he woke up. *Keeping Up with the Kardashians* was making a visit to Mount Sinai. A boom light glowed overhead as Kim gifted a signed book and tenderly stroked Jesse's cheek, nude lips heavy beneath her signature kohl-lined eyes. "Keep your pulse down," Kanye West said, as he nodded to Jesse's heart monitor. Kourtney and Khloe rearranged the floral displays. The field producer leaned against the door, making notes, a ghost haunting the hospital.

Kanye confided a story of a near-death experience he'd had as a teen: "I think about consciousness after life a lot," he said. "Like, what happens to it? Once, when I was a kid, I had a high fever, like real high, and my mom gave me some expired medicine, and I tripped. So I lay in bed sweating it out, my mom crying in a chair near me, praying. I felt like I was at my own funeral, lying there, lying there dead. I fell into total darkness, and was, like, crying out for help, in my bedroom, completely terrified, inside the darkest, blackest void I ever been inside. I'm talking total absence of, like, anything else. My mom was real scared. I try not to let myself go there, thinking on this, but that's how I think of it, when I sometimes do."

Ryan Seacrest appeared at the door, tan and grinning self-confidently. In a series of quick reaction shots it was shown that his presence has surprised even the cast. He approached the bed and shook Jesse's hand, patting his shoulder. "You're exactly the kind of fan that keeps *Keeping Up with the Kardashians* going," he said; a perfectly packaged sound bite.

"I feel so fucked up!" said Jesse. Ryan grinned again. A PR rep from the hospital stood near, keeping distance from the entire set, as if it were pestilential.

"Dedicated," he said, matter of fact. "We're all thinking of you at the network. Let us know if there is anything you need." The camera panned over Kim and Kanye, Kourtney, Khloe and Kris, each posturing meaningful frowns. Cut to Jesse rubbing tears from his wet eyes. Cut to nurse looking on fondly. Cut to Kanye with his arm around Kim. Cropped shot of Kim exhaling. Cut to the glossy cover of Kim's book, her affectless selfie peeking out behind a red ribbon, with which the thick volume had been tied.

End scene.

As the techs decamped, Jesse cleared his throat.

"Ryan, I think I have an idea for you."

"Is that right?" Ryan said, listening to a message on his phone.

"Yes," Jesse said. "It's a miniseries about a schoolmaster who moves his adolescent children from San Diego to misty Portland, Maine, after his wife goes missing during a vacation in Tijuana."

Ryan nodded, maybe listening.

"Jane Campion will clean it up and receive a co-writing credit," Jesse blurted.

Ryan scoff-laughed, looking over at the remaining cast and crew, then down again at his phone.

"It's partly about the lives of the SoCal teens, the son now using drugs, and the sister a masochist who cuts and uses sex as a distraction from her depression. The widower, the father, becomes addicted to web-camming with women who look like his late wife. Maybe Fassbender can play that role."

Ryan nodded, listening amusedly. Jesse coughed and continued.

"Well, the show turns out to be about the struggles of family. In the mini-series finale, on the one-year anniversary of her disappearance, the mother shows up to confess she left the family to disappear into happiness with a new lover. But that relationship has since failed, and in a crushing twist, she has been terminally diagnosed and wants to live with her family during her last days. So..." A few seconds passed as Jesse waited for a response.

"Well, hey, I'm genuinely impressed," Ryan said, not giving it thought. "Why weren't the cameras rolling for that?" he turned and asked no one. Jesse hoped that the crew might take the cameras back out to record another take.

"Actually, that can't air, people would hear the spoilers," Jesse said.

"Right," Ryan said, pointing at Jesse's clever realization, as if it were a thing that hung in the air between them.

"I lost my mother, similarly, a few years ago," Jesse said, telling the truth.

"I'm so sorry to hear that," Ryan said, empathically.

"Can I have your business card, so I can send you the spec script, or at least the précis?"

"Oh," Ryan relaxed and laughed. "I don't actually have a card."

"Right," Jesse said, losing energy as the visit wore on.

"Can't say I've ever received a cold pitch for a series from someone lying in a recovery room," Ryan said, with a final smile.

"But surely in bed," Jesse teased. Ryan pantomimed shock, forgiving the blue tenor of the joke.

A nurse, a fearless, petite woman who must have been close to retirement, stepped in and checked Jesse's IV. Ryan smiled and mouthed a friendly "bye," waving over his shoulder.

"Everything's more glamorous when you do it in bed," the nurse said after him, flirting with Ryan as he left, just behind the family, all escorted by the PR rep from the hospital.

A call rang up from the hospital switchboard.

"Jesse? It's your father..."

"Hey, yeah, I'm here." A dull ache radiated through his midsection, sharpened by the sound of his father's voice.

"I can't believe this, Jesse, how are you feeling? I am seconds away from stepping on a plane."

"No, don't do that, I'll be out of here soon," he lied.

"Jesse...Jesse...what have you gotten into now?" His voice was gentle but carried the potential for a lecture or admonishment.

"I'm really tired," he said, "can you call again later?"

"Are any of your friends visiting you at least?"

"Yes, tons." He couldn't stand to be loved, not now, not by his father. The call dropped, relief. There was a centering harmony felt when his bad feelings matched the impulse in his head, telling him what he deserved.

The line rang again, it was Uncle Lee. Jesse was too tired to conspire whether they were together. "Jesse, how—how are you?"

"Ummm." Jesse heard himself performing. After years under his care, he always knew what Lee was going to say; he'd always be sweet.

"How are you feeling?"

"I'm alright. I'm pretty out of it." The shock of hearing his voice was overwhelming. "Been a crazy few days."

"Well, I'm here for you." Lee was gauging Jesse's desperation. "Are you in pain?"

"No. Well, I'm on a lot of drugs." Jesse realized this wasn't the best thing to say. He could almost hear Lee frowning through the phone. "I want to come home," he pivoted.

"Alright, well your purpose now is to relax and take it easy. How long are the doctors keeping you there?"

"I'm not sure. I'm hoping to be out of here entirely in a week."

Lee paused on this. "And you've had some visitors, I suspect?"

"I feel so lonely."

"Do you want me to come visit?"

"No, no," Jesse rushed to answer. Lee didn't respond. "Well, maybe."

"Hmm, okay. Well..." Jesse heard him deciding something. "But, have you had any visitors?"

"The Kardashian family came. They recorded their visit."

"You're kidding." Lee was kind-spirited and easygoing, and had the capacity and patience to live through Jesse's turbulent teens. Lee was loyal, and expected the same; on rare occasions he turned "cunty," as Jesse had once overheard Lee confess of himself to a friend after a fight.

"No."

"That's a deeply cynical insult to injury."

"They brought a lot of ugly flowers."

"I'm so sorry, Jesse."

"My boss came from work, though."

"Oh?"

"Yeah, it was kind of weird, she kept asking how old I was, she didn't believe I was eighteen last week."

"Have you thought about signing a 'no-info' patient clause?"

"What's that?"

"Keeps people from bothering you."

"My coworkers wanted to take funny pictures with me, too. I feel so stupid now." He really did feel foolish.

"Cynicism knows no bounds. Anyways, don't worry about them."

"What was it you always said about the transcendent value of suffering?" There was a pause on the line; Jesse waited while Lee worked to get his thoughts in order.

"It's how we relate to other people. I think we always said the mark and measure of a person is their deeds, their compassion and empathy."

"Well, that really pisses me off right now."

Bernie and Patricia Shore conceived late. Jesse, their only child, was born when they were in their early 40s.

An intelligent culture enthusiast with hard features and sandy blonde hair, Patricia's easy talent for writing earned her a good living working for television, writing for daytime soaps. She became sick when Jesse was nine years old and passed a few years later, as he became a teenager. Bernie was a screenwriter, they'd met on a job ages ago. He'd left the industry and now he owned a tree-grafting and landscaping franchise.

Home life disintegrated after Patricia died. Jesse became an impossible, volatile teen, languishing inside his bedroom, curtains closed. He rarely spent time with his father, who'd remarried the spring of Jesse's senior year to an upbeat woman named Cherylene, whom Bernie called "Cher" and always introduced as an actress. Jesse scoffed at her IMDb credits, never accepting her as part of his parental unit, and scoffed again, more morbidly and desperately, each time a friend of theirs referred to them as "Bernie and Cher." He scoffed at his father's business and thrived on his own intolerance of the world at large.

Once, believing he'd heard them having sex, he went outside under the moonlight and struck the hood of her car with a folding chair, over and over, until his father, who'd been sleeping, came outside to the driveway to stop him.

Doctors blasted Jesse with SSRIs. Benzodiazepines held day-to-day life steady. He ran long distance track to escape, took drugs to dim his mind, skipped school, grew to his father's height, five feet ten inches. He had his father's jet-black hair, his mother's shocking blue eyes.

In her last years, his mother created and developed a semi-autobiographical primetime miniseries called *Until I See Palm Trees Again*, an unassuming but dense show detailing the final months of a mother's life cut short by a fast-coming disease. She passed away while the show was in post-production.

Until I See Palm Trees Again was written for Jesse, though he had never seen it. He'd actively avoided doing so, though he'd imagined a copy was in his family's possession when he was ready. The show was a critical, if not commercial, success, with moderate viewership. The series was shot almost entirely on location using natural lighting and had a visual atmosphere and mood that was, until then, exclusively reserved for cinema. Patricia was nominated for an Emmy for Outstanding Writing for a Miniseries (losing to Tony Kushner's *Angels in America* miniseries adaptation).

His only sanctuary in these years were solitary drives to visit his Uncle Lee, his mother's gay brother. It was Lee, not his father, who attended the Emmys with Jesse as representatives. An image of the two of them in tuxedos touched lives across the nation when the cameras cut to the two of them, neatly seated in their row. The Television Academy printed and framed the image, which Bernie displayed prominently in their home, though the fact of its presence began to supplant him as head of the nuclear family, with Lee now the icon of a newer order, a patron of the child.

Wholesale rejection of his father was a necessary cost of moving forward from the loss of his mother. Jesse spent as much time at Uncle Lee's as he could, skipping school to smoke weed in the shade by the pool, binge television and stay up all night watching movies from their impressive film library.

He received his aesthetic education in this second home. The on-screen narratives he worshiped became the organizing principle of his existence; well-rendered fictions held the best representation of the world as he actively experienced it, one of tragedy, with its mutable values, its reversals and contradictions.

Why are narratives so True, he often daydreamed the question. *They are so satisfying; a good story. The "tale as old as time." The "fool's journey." The grail quest. The Italian passion films. Swedish winter light.* The only fight he'd ever seen his parents have was over this same struggle. Were there a limited number of stories? When he recalled the specifics of the fight, it was the timbre and passion his mother showed that he recalled—he couldn't have said who was on which side, though either was affirmed by the effort.

Jesse deferred going to UCLA to study screenwriting—the only idea he had for his future—but instead went to NYC, for a gap year, on his uncle's orders.

He'd been there a year, a relatively steady life of working full time, hanging out with the few acquaintances he'd made at his job, blowing his paycheck on clothes and cab rides. Los Angeles, Lee's connections and the industry, would always be there for him. Spring in New York had been disappointingly brief this year. He'd suffered his first Northeast winter, and in the interval of high romanticism, when the pear trees bloomed and the drugged scent of semen and sex occupied the avenues, when the afternoons were bright with something more than sunlight, those days seemed to apprehend the divine, and slowed the urgency of summer.

Lying in Mount Sinai in the anxious aftermath of the tragedy of his pending television cameo, he regretted the wrecked pitch he'd given for the show he'd not quite entirely thought through during idle time folding clothes at the store, or during stalled commutes, never putting it onto paper, never thinking he'd need to formally work out a pitch. He felt so lonely, the acquaintances and hookups and tenuous friendships he'd created in the last year suddenly melted into air. The hospital room machinery continued its indifferent mechanics. He missed anything familiar, the songs he loved, Uncle Lee, then suddenly felt very far from his mother. He sank down so far into an isolated despair, an adolescent fantasia set in, where he believed she could appear at the door at any moment.

Daytime soaps were on. He often thought about the texture of the language of show titles like *Days of Our Lives*, or *One Life to Live*, *As the World Turns*, and included his mother's own show among these lush and melancholy phrases. He thought of the melancholic veneer that coated the days of his own life, and the truth of the way to use a life cloaked him with a new resolve. He could—truly would—become a screenwriter like his mother and commit to her legacy by creating work in her honor, in all its realization. His attempts at better living since her death had amounted to a series of idle, empty gestures, but now he believed he'd better give them at least half a try.

He closed his eyes and imagined writing the kinds of transpersonal fictions he loved. The contemporary affect-flows that rock a group of incommensurate but closely connected characters, maybe a family and their kind; the alluring and desperate struggles of lives lived too short or too long, overstuffed with hard situations, impossible loves. He'd respond to emails from the production team on Uncle Lee's sun-blasted patio, near the pool, working on plotlines while listening to music and daydreaming, nursing a silly crush on someone he'd just met, and enjoying the passing time.

He meditated before an imagined altar to the writers he wanted to be, would become, would overtake: Aaron Sorkin, Tina Fey, J.J. Abrams, their masterful storylines, their world-building, the breathtaking final shots before the credits rolled. He thought of the writing that fueled serial television, speculation scripts, whiteboards in the writing room. On film the director was on top, but on TV the writer was the auteur. *A brilliant new golden age has dawned for me*, he agreed to himself, half-mouthing the words in his hospital bed. His mind turned to the afterword the network had added to *Until I See Palm Trees Again*, which appeared beneath an image of his mother his uncle had printed and framed on their wall:

"Perhaps this is not a story at all and yet I think it is. Is life ever definite in its answer; is the story ever really finished? We can, all of us, imagine things to come after the end of a story, be the story our own or that of some other."

Charles Demuth

He meditated on the narratives that had informed his studies in the past:

The survivors of a plane crash are forced to work together in order to survive on a seemingly deserted tropical island.

The trials and tribulations of small town Texas football players, their friends, family and coaching staff.

Follows the lives of six twenty-something friends living in Manhattan.

A young girl, destined to slay vampires, demons and other infernal creatures, deals with her life fighting evil, with the help of her friends.

A hot-tempered farm laborer convinces the woman he loves to marry their dying boss so they can have a claim to his fortune.

An LA family with serious boundary issues has their past and future unravel when a dramatic admission causes everyone's secrets to spill out.

A failed writer pens a screenplay for a former silent-film star who has faded into Hollywood obscurity.

Detective Robin Griffin begins a dangerous investigation of her hometown's secrets after a pregnant twelve-year-old attempts suicide in a freezing New Zealand lake.

The absurd antics of an Indiana town's public officials as they pursue sundry projects to make their city a better place.

Four girls hold up a restaurant in order to fund their college vacation.

A passionless actor reexamines his life when his eleven-year-old daughter surprises him with a visit to his West Hollywood hotel residence.

A mentally unstable Vietnam veteran works as a night-time taxi driver in New York City.

A self-diagnosed nymphomaniac recounts her erotic experiences to the man who saved her after a beating.

A darkly comical look at members of a dysfunctional California family that runs an independent funeral home.

Media released Jesse's name the following morning, listed alongside the other survivor and the deceased. Both gun control and gun rights advocates were reaching out for comment, message endorsements and sponsorships. His inboxes were full. Tabloid interns flooded his social media to fact-check. An unpopular daytime talk show in the UK had invited him to make a video appearance.

A nurse entered, rolling a dinner cart. Jesse raised his bed up. He'd had no fever and was able to digest food with no problems. Good signs by the doctor's telling.

His primary doctor came in with a clipboard holding forms. He'd be released within forty-eight hours. He was presented a pamphlet about incision care: how to sponge-bathe the stitching and lightly pat it down after showering, how to brace during a cough to prevent the wound from reopening. How to inspect for signs of infection.

"As far as pain, I'm going to prescribe a few days worth of hydrocodone..." His tone had the assured sense of someone doing a favor and not taking objections.

Jesse broke in, "I'm not sure I'd want that."

"Now, don't play the tough guy, Jesse, this is a serious injury. Rest is the key to recovery."

"Look," Jesse said. "A few years ago I would have crushed that prescription and sucked it up my nose." The doctor's demeanor tightened. "I'm trying to keep my shit together here."

"Okay, so we've had a problem."

"I want those pills, but I can't."

"These are actually crush-resistant," the doctor said, setting the pen down. "Are you actively using other drugs?"

"No, that's all behind me."

"I'm going to write the prescription, just for a few days, just so you have it. No mixing with alcohol, of course."

Jesse had been something of a demon in those years of abandon. Just after his mother died, his father had been detached enough, buttressed by SSRIs and sleeping pills, that he indulged any boyish caprice his son wished. At age twelve, Jesse became nocturnal, avoiding times of the day his mother's absence felt strongest, sleeping after school, well past midnight, then eating Count Chocula and Lucky Charms while watching TV until it was time again for class in the morning. Once Bernie shook the low ceiling of cloud cover that had mummified his judgment, he began asserting himself as an authority, chafing against the liberty Jesse had settled into just as he became a teenager facing down puberty and all its contradictory clauses. Burdened by grief and fatigue, temperatures swelled between them as their relationship deteriorated. Shouting in the house became common. At fourteen he'd first had his stomach pumped of liquor. Age fifteen he spent taking drugs and learning to drive. Age sixteen he totaled his car and got a DUI, in broad daylight, with no memory of any of it. Age seventeen was spent living almost exclusively at "The Chateau," Lee's home, in ascetic constraint, breathing through the television screen as support for sobriety. At eighteen he moved to New York.

"Do you want me to have a social worker or counselor come in to speak about outpatient support for—"

"No."

The doctor tidied his papers and stood up.

"Good luck." He reached towards Jesse and they shook hands. But Jesse wasn't present for it. He was deciding to quit his job, sorting his belongings in his head, tossing them to the street.

On day twelve, just before Jesse was released, a nurse loaned him an iPad. He leaned up on one shoulder, brushed away the dirty hair from his face, and typed *Jesse + Shore + Kim + Kardashian* into the search bar.

If being the son of Patricia Shore had introduced him to a small industry set in greater Los Angeles, being named by the media as a survivor of a public shooting surrounding such a high-profile figure was making him temporarily famous. His photo, taken from one of his online profiles, was broadcast on television and online in news stories. In the picture he was on the roof of a Lower East Side hotel, succulents and stucco from the retaining walls behind him, black-and-white patio umbrellas beneath the huge blue sky beyond. It was a gorgeous arrangement of scenery and Jesse recognized himself attempting to outdo it.

Thousands of people had followed him online, he suspected mostly to gawk. He tweeted "I'm ok," adding a smiley face that was wearing sunglasses, but deleted it. He tried again: "I'm ok because I met @KimKardashian," adding two smiley faces, both wearing sunglasses, then deleted that too. He'd written half another tweet before redirecting his attention to profiles of the other victims. Marsy-Rose Arenas, whose profile said only "Overeducated, mixed-race, aspiring actress: LA & NYC," had been grazed in the shoulder and released from the hospital on the same day. Jesse meditated distantly on the smaller image of the deceased, a thirty-two-year-old woman who was pictured jumping mid-air, a photo frivolously snapped on the beach for posterity while on vacation.

His attention went back to Marsy-Rose. He felt helpless before the allure of her profile picture; she had a brushed porcelain complexion, smoky almond eyes, big, thick eyebrows, her mouth held delicately open in the photo. A plunging V-neck dress accentuated the minimal curves of her thin frame. She wore heavy makeup and took the photo from a practiced angle to make her dark lashes and pout pop.

Marsy-Rose Arenas had a tremendous number of followers, nearly six digits, and to his surprise and delight he saw she had recently followed him. He followed her back and began reading her tweets.

"Convalescing," one said, above a picture of her feet, manicured toenails over color-saturated water.

"Passengers, we are now beginning our descent home to LA," another said, with a photo of the greater Southern California coastline.

Jesse mused over this while glancing disinterestedly at messages from the high school acquaintances he cared little for, thoughtful notes from random internet strangers, and other solicitations that had accumulated in his direct message box.

He started a message to Marsy-Rose, typing a note saying "hi" and pressing send. He returned to her profile, feeling as if he'd already been set up on a blind date. He dwelled lustfully over the hope of a short, bright-burning romance, then tucked the reverie away, as he had hundreds if not thousands of times already in his life, in the privacy of his own fantasies, feeling foolish and embarrassed when he didn't immediately hear back.

He opened the message thread and impulsively added a heart as follow-up, thinking it was in solidarity with their recently shared tragedy, then regretted it, realizing it was a slip back from behavioral therapy training that taught reflection against reaction, patience instead of rash misdirection, anger management, solutions to the milieu of bad behaviors he'd developed in the big shadow of his mother's passing. He shut the tablet off and looked for the nurse. He was hungry, his body off the hospital feeding schedule, a sign it was time to go.

At home in the small studio where he lived alone, he listed his possessions for sale online, all of them out of place in the new life he was already living in his head. He took a long shower, alone with his body for the first time in a week, inspecting his tender pink scar, a new companion, then ordered heaps of Chinese food while looking at flights out of New York.

He returned to his online correspondence. A girl from work he'd been fucking had sent a warm note expressing everyone's disbelief over what had happened, offering to help however she could. Lee had written back to his travel queries, ending his email by asking if he had reached out to his father. Jesse dodged, feeling guilty he hadn't, though the guilt turned to anger he'd been made to feel obliged. He looked at messages on Twitter as an easy distraction. Marsy-Rose had responded:

Hey there, pretty, it's nice to finally meet you. I had been meaning to reach out when I saw the stories about us, but I've been swamped. Looks like you've been through a lot. Let's have coffee one day, when you can. Get well soon. Yours, Mars

Mars. He searched her name online, found her personal website and studied her long list of small-role acting appearances, her moderate modeling credentials.

Other results showed her photographed several times with her boyfriend, the actor Marc Pevier, a name Jesse knew from the cringe-inducing HBO show *Retinue*, a comedy about a film star fucking around with his entourage. An article in *Media Takeout* reported Marc had recently been spotted at a New York club with an unknown teenage girl, though Jesse couldn't verify that with his own eyes, squinting at the blurry pictures. He read an article suggesting Marc had a history of being caught with eighteen- and nineteen-year-olds. The photo, however, featured him and Mars in front of a red carpet step-and-repeat, as if she, too, was a teen he'd dashed off with for a weekend getaway, charmed by his easy-going fame, his effortless handsomeness. Jesse hated him. He read snippets of articles about her, everything he could find; more than a dozen tabs opened. He looked through what must have been two hundred pictures, professionally posed, likely retouched. He felt overpowered by their suggestions of arch command or brutal dominion or good sex. When he wrote back to Mars, it was with renewed determination to get back to the West Coast as soon as possible.

Chapter 2: Until I See Palm Trees Again

Jesse'd kept in touch with Mars the week before he left for Los Angeles, and when his plane broke the cloud line it was as if the whole nation knew something seismic was about to happen between them.

On the plane he found a copy of *Fifty Shades of Grey* in the seatback pocket, bookmarked on page ten and otherwise unread. In preparation for six hours of boredom, he'd downloaded a TV series onto his computer, but in the context of the flight he'd lost his taste. He scrolled through the films available for purchase, and found *Fifty Shades of Grey*. He swiped his card.

Jesse knew from chats with Lee that the film's adaptation was one of the most coveted screenwriting jobs to come to Hollywood in years. Kelly Marcel, an acquaintance of Lee's who was hired for the job, left the project disenfranchised, saying she wouldn't return for the second film.

Like seaglass rubbed until it's lost its cruel edge, the film landed somewhere further from erotica and closer to a love story with a gloomy windup. Jesse became bored and pressed the "X" icon to stop the film on the tiny screen. He stabbed the cubes of ice with the thin red straw and considered ordering another seltzer, then coffee, but instead scrolled through apps on his phone. He bought the Ellie Goulding song from the movie's soundtrack on iTunes and added it to its own repeating playlist containing just that song. He felt rapacious and closed his eyes, thinking again of Mars.

As the song throbbed and peaked in his earbuds, their rendezvous seemed more pressing and urgent. He anxiously drafted a new message, asking to meet that evening, and sent it over, immediately regretting it. His stomach ached the more he dwelled on it; now he wanted the muscle relaxers he'd said no to. He'd been sitting down for hours and looked on enviously at his neighbor's well-planned package of sleep aids, earplugs, sunglasses and an organic neck pillow. He curled up with himself, hands inside his t-shirt, and finally slept.

When he woke up they were making their descent into the Angeleno sunset. Jesse had forgotten about the Calabasas fires, which had been raging for the better part of the week. A large plume of smoke hung just below the cloud line, the sky streaked melon and orange. *Love Me Like You Do* had been playing in his headphones for hours.

He'd made it home.

He'd almost forgotten how bright Southern California was, pushing sunshine down your throat until you gagged. Sun over waves. Sun over glass. Sun in the wines. Sun over succulents. Sun over reruns. Sun on traffic. Sun over dramas and desperations and timid hookups and last breaths. Sun over skid row. Sunshine over rehab. Sun over cell towers. Sun on dispensaries. Sun pouring over sun. Sunshine blasting the closed set. Sun buying drugs. January wave. Cars overheating in traffic.

Lee had a last-minute business dinner he'd taken as a favor and couldn't pick Jesse up from LAX. A potential client, as he'd described him, was eating with him in his home in Echo Park, and Jesse was to call a car—he was looking forward to seeing him, of course—and he could cover the cost of the ride.

Sunsets in New York signified the closing of the daily commercial cycle, a budget-friendly reward for a day's work. Sunsets over Southern California seemed closer to heaven, a bonnet over a sleepy province of ticking desperations.

Jesse loved seeing palm trees at night, spellbound by their indifferent sway. Riding beneath their grand fronds, which blistered above the halogen lamplight, the blood-red sky eased into darkness as he switched his focus to his phone, where he watched the pillish blue GPS dot on the map also going for a cruise. The meditation was interrupted by a *Los Angeles Times* alert saying a shallow-magnitude earthquake had just occurred in Joshua Tree. He set the phone down in his lap, letting the backlight redouble in the car window.

As with any homecoming, Jesse became filled with pathos and melancholy as he rode along the defamiliarized geography. He rubbed his fingers over his scar—an anxious habit he'd developed—as butterflies rose and fell in his chest. It was now night and traffic was moderate. Neither he nor the driver spoke. The radio dialed in information about accidents on the freeways. The 110 was down to one lane near

The Staples Center, causing a two-mile backup; the driver took the 405 to the 10. They exited to bypass delays from a stalled vehicle.

The residential strips on Venice Boulevard patiently proffered aloe vera, blooming bougainvillea and wild roses while odd memories settled. The street of a girl with whom he'd taken edibles: they'd gotten awfully stoned, and a day later she'd desperately looked up "high forever." They'd never spoken since. Once, his father had taken him to The Grove to a movie, and Jesse went to use the restroom and simply walked out into hard sun instead, fueled by rage, defiantly running for blocks towards his mother's burial plot, eventually becoming lost in Beverly Hills in the afternoon, when landscapers were the only people outdoors.

"The solitary life Jesse had led of late, and the melancholy subjects on which he had suffered his thoughts to dwell, had rendered him at times susceptible to the 'thick-coming fancies' of a mind newly enervated." Since the shooting, he'd been living in quotations, as if drawn into a narrative steered by higher powers. He'd also been flirting with a "what does it all mean" moment, the eternal return of horrible feelings he hadn't felt possessed by since his mother passed. When he first processed his mother's death, in therapy, he told of a recurring dream of a cloaked figure hung above the foot of his bed. He frequently woke himself to shouts and cries, as if there were something to be fought with there. A shadow self of him had died alongside his mother, and he learned to ask what that iteration needed, how to love him. The flood of emotions the technique required settled now anew. He'd also been riding the bombastic high of being reported on in the news, all that frenetic attention. He could be recognized by anyone at any time.

Lee built his house, The Chateau, in Angelino Heights, 2005, and as Jesse pulled onto Carroll Avenue past the Victorian manors and familiar fan palms, he indulged the nostalgia of the paradise he'd made of it when he was younger. The house was 4,600 square feet and had plenty of space: two full living rooms with fireplaces, a dining room, kitchen, hot tub, pool, private gardens and secluded terraces. It was painted soft green with white trim, ironically stately and awkward among the legacy homes around it.

The home was something of a gay domestic haven, an enviable wreath of Lee's fortunes. Too personal to be used as an income tool through popular rental outlets, the well-tended grounds inflected the specific and separate character of its owner.

The Chateau was also something of a stage actor's paradise, each room having taken on the quality of a set, the kitchen with its permanent rotation of tidy place settings, glinting counters, blooming orchids, overflowing bowls of fruit.

The art hung in the hall spilled into the living room, and was a highlight of visiting The Chateau. An image of Anthony Andrews holding a teddy bear from *Brideshead Revisited* appeared next to solemn signed stills of Kathy Griffin and Regis Philbin. The photo of Jesse and Lee in tuxedos at the Emmys was framed in a less-than-earnest gauche gilt frame. It was their "Celeb Wall," as they called it, though the moniker was cheeky, and all of the featured stars were friends or acquaintances: Juliette Binoche, Naomi Watts, Johnny Depp, Meryl Streep, Cate Blanchett, Gregg Araki, Adrien Brody, Henry Fonda, Dustin Hoffman, Gregory Peck, Robert Altman, Liza Minnelli, Cher, Jodie Foster, Shirley MacLaine, Ingrid Bergman, Sydney Pollack. The fact of the installation itself occasioned gifts, and finally, when Hal Ashby gave Lee a signed color snapshot of Marilyn Monroe (white stole, black halter) on his fortieth birthday, they considered the installation finished.

Lee's office was rarely shown, carpeted in a deep, halting high-pile red, and several models of the Queen Elizabeth Luxury Liner sat near his desk in a glass vitrine, leftover from a high-camp show he'd worked on that was set at sea. He'd installed a modest chandelier, hung gold frames on the soft yellow walls.

Jesse had claimed the entire downstairs floor, which opened at the back to the pool, as living quarters. Its open plan included a cavernous interior of leather and various neon lights. The design was inspired by Lee's first experiences with sexuality he'd had in a vicious and bawdy leather club in Budapest in the 1980s.

After finding the house empty, he located Lee sitting out back beneath the lamps that delineated the edge of the porch from the beginning of the deck around the pool. Lee looked as Jesse remembered, slim and short with a petite swimmer's frame, wearing a short-sleeved button up and white shorts. More gray swarmed his trim stubble and hairline. Someone Jesse couldn't place sat with him, soft-faced with pale skin, and dressed in all black. His hair was dyed incompatibly black for his age, his youthfully messy mop swept over his head, a look complicated by thin-rimmed glasses.

Lee introduced the man as Brian. They were both drinking absinthe, which seemed odd to Jesse. Brian was in development with a French video game company.

"They screened their last game at Cannes, put Willem Dafoe and Elliot Page in front of a green screen," he said, teasing the glass from one angle to another, so his ice tinkled in a circle. "We're talking about a huge budget. They had Hans Zimmer do that soundtrack. I'm going to do this one myself though, or maybe bring in some collaborators. That's what all the big players are doing now." He had a blunt arrogance, an industry overconfidence filtered through a West Coast fry. "Look, we're talking 30 million," he said with finality, as if that fact alone would guarantee interest, which it did. "We give them a great story, and they develop the sensible, functional game mechanics for us."

He explained that years ago he'd developed a fantasy horror film that languished in post-production. He was repackaging it as a video game narrative. He wanted Lee to continue developing the story and suggested Lee shoot live-action scenes in his signature dream-sequence style.

"I want the fucked psychological feeling, in the horror genre," he said. "I want Eli Roth goes to *The Beach*, Michael Haneke does *House of a Thousand Corpses*. All mixed with a horrible theater of paranormal activities. An M. Night Shyamalan drama of uncertainty and suspense, but the twist is that the world is more fucked up than we're comfortable to admit, that horror is in reality. Reality is the scariest thing. I want to demonstrate that."

"A participatory *Funny Games*," Lee said, looking over the glinting inflections of the pool, "which, as you know, I shot."

"For sure, no doubt, no doubt," Brian said.

As they talked, Jesse slowly realized he was speaking with Marilyn Manson. Though he knew Lee to take a meeting out of politeness, he also followed serious money as much as aesthetic compatibility, and it seemed like here, there could be a lot. His thought was to convince them to pass the job down to him, or for Lee to allow him to co-write, imagining this as a launch pad to Real Hollywood.

"Wait, I know you, right?" Brian said then, leaning forward and focusing intently on Jesse, who felt locked in the scope of attention. "Dude, you were, like, shot, right?" Lee paled. Jesse looked over the bottle of absinthe, the pool's sentient quivering. It was the first time he felt forced to take ownership of the incident.

"Yeah," Jesse said, leaning back and lifting his shirt. Lee recoiled as Brian examined the small slash upon his thin frame, his body otherwise coated in a thin layer of Virgin Airlines particulate. Then he turned around, showing him the exit wound, craning his neck to get a view himself. There was less to see on his lower back, a wartish pink polyp near his waistline. Lee's face soured as he squinted to bring the wounds into focus. Jesse felt sickened that he'd shown himself off this way and decided never to do it again.

"We should talk sometime. Actually, I'd like to get your perceptions of the horror present in said scenario. I was thinking this game would start in media res, you know like, you choose one of several characters whose story collides and refracts with the others."

Jesse went inward, thinking of Mars, turning her name over in his head, Marsy-Rose Arenas, then thought of the hospital, the unknowable dead technician, then his late mother. When she passed, he was told she went to heaven, but that comfort faded like a rose. It was the two-week anniversary of the shooting, and here the industry was already absorbing the narrative, novelizing it for popular consumption, showing little of the outrage that was present when Christina Grimmie had been similarly murdered. Jesse felt naïve in his smugness that he could master the narratives in his life. The trio sat in extended silence.

"Well, maybe you could co-write it, or get an advisory credit. That's something that could be great for this project, don't you think?" Brian asked Lee.

"Maybe," Lee frowned. "To imagine is to see." Jesse perked at this. The phrase was a sure tell Lee wasn't interested; he said it when the answer was going to be no.

Brian finished his drink and slowly stood. They shook hands and Lee saw Brian out through a squeaky side gate. Jesse stood over the rippling water, the quiet of the night, the gauche glass of absinthe the remainder of the evening, until Lee returned.

"It's really good to see you," Lee said, rubbing Jesse's shoulder. Jesse leaned in for a sort of side-hug, which they held tight for a moment.

"Do screenwriters really write video games?" Jesse was skeptical. Lee laughed.

"Yes, actually, it's a huge market." Jesse wanted badly to ask the next question, but balked. "I have so little interest in this, it's all yours," Lee said, to Jesse's satisfaction. "But that stays between us," he added firmly. "Write the précis, consider it practice, if it's good," he paused, "I'll say we co-wrote it, and pass it on." Jesse offered to clean up. Lee patted him on the back again then went inside. It was the most touched Jesse had felt in months.

The air smelled like fennel and chlorine. A sudden jolt of melancholy rippled through his nervous system. He stared at the small amount of liquor calmly stirring about the tumbler, wondering what would happen if he drank it; he'd been dry from alcohol for years. He felt exhausted, emotionally wrecked, conditions he'd been warned lead to getting drunk. He held it to his nose, recoiling from the sweet burn that rushed through his nostrils.

He sat with his feet in the water and looked on his phone for messages from Mars. Their meeting was imminent, as soon as tomorrow. He'd extrapolated a lot from the pictures she'd posted online. She occasionally worked as a spokesperson, she had a robust modeling portfolio and healthy active lifestyle: not just relatable, but likeable, the winning type of limited liability persona people feel comfortable putting their reputation and money behind.

He felt humiliated by his crush and embarrassed of his optimism. He found there, however, something to be excited about. He lifted the glass and admired the emerald color, burying his nose a second time, inhaling deep into his lungs. Instead he poured it into the pool, laying back, looking up at the sky over Echo Park, Los Angeles, California, the only Truth of existence being a composite of cellular material, held together in a wounded body, however temporarily, in space, in time, an organism that persisted, the whole of his sense of self now returned to the town of our lady, queen of the angels, splendidly, as it were.

Did you make it to LA?

Yes, I did

And what are you up to?

I'm starving

Me too what are you gonna eat? Where do you live?

Echo Park, you?

Lincoln Heights, near my family. I'm in Highland Park now, though.

For work?

Nah

That's cool

Yeah, don't ask me to go to the west side unless it's for sex or I'm being paid. A lot. Wait how did you find a place so fast?

I'm living with my uncle, actually, for I'm-not-sure-how-long
Gonna have that awkward convo soon

I'm craving good Mexican food, no offense NYC

I saw a picture of a taco truck
in those travel catalogs in the plane
they had a feature on LA food

That's embarrassing lol
Which truck?

I know urgh sorry. It's called um Tacos something

Yeah I know that one!
actually it's really fucking good and
I would like to go with you when you go, Jesse Shore.

Uh, yeah, sure? Like today?
I guess I better figure out how to get myself out of bed

SORRY. I won't message at 9am again :-)

HAHA.
It's ok if you are inviting me to things

Well I want to meet you. When did you get back?

Last night. Already got a writing offer actually

Look at you

Chapter 3: Torn at the Edge

Mars was sitting on the trunk of her Ford Focus with her feet on the bumper when Jesse arrived. A sudden flash of nerves manifested a chill upon his spine. She wore false lashes, a crop top and a tremendous engagement ring. She had huge contoured cheekbones and a small mouth set beneath slanting, big eyes.

Jesse had on a gray pocket t-shirt and jeans he'd had custom-made at work.

The truck was stationed at the edge of a parking lot, and they stood in line making small talk over topics they'd already discussed over text: which neighborhoods they lived in, how their travel back to LA had been, how long they'd been back. Southern California had been in a drought, and a storm was finally passing through the region. The sky was growing overcast, filling with silver puffs, backlit by the supernal power of the sun. They walked back to her car, using her dirty trunk as a tabletop after they got their food.

"Did you know they're blowing molecules into the clouds?"

"Why?" Jesse asked, self-consciously tilting his head for a bite of taco.

"The drought. It's called cloud-seeding, they time it with the storms to make it rain more."

"Studio magic."

"Post-production, for sure."

Jesse nervously stabbed pork out of his tacos with a fork. Mars took a few wolfish bites then seemingly forgot about the meal altogether. He looked at her when she wasn't looking, wondering what it was she was here for. A fit couple dressed to go hiking ate beside them in the open back of an SUV. The woman—headband, high ponytail—asked if she recognized Mars from a recent story on TMZ. Mars responded to her candidly, in a friendly tone, as if she were a celebrity being sighted, and in a sense, she was. She asked if Mars and Jesse were a couple as the dog towed her partner away, tugging the leash, studying squirrels.

"Amor fati," Mars said ambiguously. She flashed her eyes at Jesse, batting her lashes a few times. He looked at her ring finger again, feeling the complicated pride that she would claim him as a lover.

"Oh, like *The Hunger Games*," the woman said, glaring down her freckled nose.

"Are you Ryan Morgan Hart?" Mars suddenly asked, accusingly, at the woman's partner. She turned back to Jesse, saying just loudly enough, "He's a personal trainer, you know, the kind who goes for in-home appointments in Calabasas and the Hills. Rumor is he sold pictures of a client for tons of cash."

The woman turned away in disgust.

"And guess who got fired, the Latino gardeners," she called after them. The man confirmed his identity by raising a middle finger over his shoulder, not looking back.

"What just happened?" Jesse said.

"Forget it," Mars said, checking her phone and taking a sip of her tall bottle of Jarritos. Jesse felt a paranoid wave that the shooting and subsequent attention were part of a Faustian deal Mars had made to become more famous by way of the incident, he and the dead woman the collateral damage of her career path.

"Want some?" Mars asked, sliding the bottle over to Jesse. He did.

There was lipstick on the straw and he tentatively took a few sips, relaxing into the day, his new environment, and a nascent friendship, this stranger before him.

"My uncles work as gardeners. They're the most expendable, lowest-class citizens, and fools like him know that." Mars was unfolding her sunglasses and checking herself in their reflection. Jesse meditated on her small shoulders and lavender nails, her slight torso and full brown hair. She then looked up coyly at Jesse, inspecting him for the first time. He watched her looking back at him, their eyes crossing paths, locking in and out. What she saw, she didn't comment on.

"What do you want to do now?" she asked.

Jesse had no idea, but whatever it was she wanted, he was going to do it. He looked at her engagement ring again, though decided against asking about it.

"Do you want to come watch Big Daddy give me some injections?"

"I'm...not following you?" he said.

"Big Daddy is my doctor. He gives me fillers. And then we'll go by a dispensary? Need more lotion to manage the pain." She said the last words as if repeating an ad. She pulled her shirt off her shoulder, turning her back to Jesse. Her own fresh pink scar, a violent streak of stubbed baby skin, was raised delicately on her smooth skin. There was a thin tan line. "I've been reading a lot of scar-healing testimonials. I'm starting treatment next week, actually. I've been meaning to do it, for my face, you know, at my age you need it, so they roll a bunch of tiny needles over scars or old skin to create little holes and collagen builds back in there. It's like creating new flesh, or something."

"More studio magic?"

"Sci-fi makeup trailer, for sure."

"Let me see," she said, using her hand to call forth his actions, like a conductor. He straightened his posture and raised his shirt.

His scars were as unattractive and garish as Mars'. She opened her handbag and removed several wound maturation products: Mederma, ScarGuard, tea tree oil, garlic oil.

"I didn't even know there was a market for scar healing," Jesse said, feeling self-conscious as he raised his shirt, though this time it meant something different, and he felt safe. He almost wondered aloud if the same bullet had hit them both, and nearly suggested it. He began feeling quite alone again and a rush of isolation flooded his chest and throat.

"Yeah, there's a market for everything, hunno," Mars said.

She squirted baby formula Aquaphor moisturizer into her hand, and then added a few drops of vitamin E oil. She turned and stood in front of him as he sat on the trunk of her car, his legs dangling towards the gravel. He raised his t-shirt again and she applied the balm gently to his abdomen, their first touch, under the shelter of live oaks as a light rain began to fall in a Walgreens parking lot that also serviced customers of Lassen's Natural Foods and a Little Caesar's. A stream of convertibles zipped down Sunset, followed by an empty TMZ bus. She rubbed the excess lotion onto her shoulder before dumping the cosmetics back into her handbag. "Take this," she said. It was a CBD lotion. He studied the label: *antiseptic, analgesic, and anti-inflammatory. CBD has no "high" or psychoactive effect. Legal in all 50 states!*

"That's Megan Fox," she said. "You see that white car?"

"No?"

"Right there at the end." Mars nodded her head.

Jesse saw a woman sitting in a small BMW, a compact SUV, a natural choice for someone trying to comfortably lower their profile. A woman Jesse's age, likely her assistant, was carrying a green juice and a clear plastic container full of greens toward the car. If it were Megan Fox, he wouldn't have recognized her on his own. Megan was skimming something, flipping through pages, and Jesse imagined she was reading a script.

He thought of all the work he needed to do on stories he'd not yet thought of. "There are rich stories wherever people are," he'd once heard Lee say.

"Gotta love her in those *Transformers* movies, right? A family film where father and son are secretly thinking of banging her."

"Totally," Jesse scoffed. They watched the woman balance the juice as she opened the door, handing the beverage into the car before sitting down in the driver's seat. "God, the last movie I watched with my dad was, um," he stared into the gray sky above the strip and waited for the truth to come to mind. "One of the *Spiderman* films."

"Tobey Maguire or Andrew Garfield?"

"Definitely Tobey Maguire. I dumped my dad before the reboots."

"Why?"

"It's emotional, I don't know. Can a son really square with his father?" His reasoning was immature, and he hoped he wouldn't have to explain more. He knew the truth, a year of clarity in New York had given him clear answers; he'd demanded to be a victim, using his absence as a weapon to cause pain in his father's life.

"I hate my dad," Mars said.

"Whoa, why?" Jesse asked, eager for an answer. Mars squirmed a moment, scratching at her shoulder.

"He's an asshole," she said, "a handsome, sort-of intellectual, never knocked the chip off his own shoulder about the things he couldn't do in life. He's always getting fired, changing jobs. Plus my mom's a clinical narcissist."

The thought hung in the air between them.

"Let's take a picture," Mars then said. She seemed above taking a picture of Megan Fox in workout clothes in a parking lot surrounded by bus stops, but when Mars lifted her phone, she flipped the camera back toward them.

Jesse slid down from Mars' Focus and she lifted her phone up, changing angles and arm position until they had good light and a decent background. She turned toward Jesse and pushed her lips out, he stood as close to her as decorum would allow. They took a few pictures and Mars swiped through to review them.

"This is a good one of you, I'm going to post this," she said, shoving the phone into Jesse's face. In the photo he radiated towards the lens. Mars looked great, her face blank in the suggestive style of the zeitgeist. They looked cute. A drop of water hit the screen.

"I love it when it rains here," Mars said.

"I was actually looking forward to some stability," Jesse said. Mars turned to him, smiling.

The wind picked up and water dripped onto them from the shaking branches.

"Ok, let's get ourselves to Big Daddy's!"

Jesse followed Mars in his car out of the parking lot as rain continued falling. Warped and melted from summer, the windshield wipers lunked along the glass as he scanned through radio stations. There are no second acts in American lives, sure, but Bieber's *Love Yourself* was on, and Jesse recalled the performance at the MTV Video Music Awards, where Bieber had presented new songs and cried at the audience's maniacal support. The song was a café-cut suited for a Caribou or Tully's or a CD sold at Starbucks.

Britney Spears' *Till The World Ends* came on after that. The end of the world was overdone.

The song rang against the scrape of the wipers, and Jesse let it play as the drizzle blurred his vision. He studied the semiotics of Mars' license plate: 5ALN015. He knew it was randomly generated and couldn't mean anything, though the red California script font lent lasciviousness to the car just because it was hers. His adoration of it, too, was immediate.

Watching her car, taking traffic cues from the dance of her brake lights, it was a mindless exercise, imagining potentialities for world ending, envisioning a high-definition comet storm was careening towards Sunset Boulevard right then. He saw the first fireball eclipsing the San Gabriel ridgeline, firebombing through In-N-Out and burrowing into the street before him, sending up earth and steel and concrete, compacting Mars' car against the hillside, her body and essence crushed with this galactic extinction event.

His phone rang, breaking the spell. It was a California number he didn't recognize. When he answered, it was Mars. He put her on speaker and set the phone face-up on the console.

"Hey, sorry to call, but my car is doing this thing where the battery slowly dies. I got stranded because of this yesterday. Dammit."

Never having heard her in distress before, Jesse didn't recognize her voice and struggled to find her in the conversation.

"So what do you want to do?"

"Let's see if we can get to Big Daddy's, if not, I don't even know, man." The stress in her voice was something new.

They were only a few minutes from the doctor's office. Jesse followed her into the parking lot. When she turned off her car, it wouldn't start again. She cautiously opened the car door, not letting rain in. They huddled and Mars crouched under Jesse's arm, running into the entrance of the doctor's office.

"Mars?!" the receptionist shrieked gleefully.

"Oh my god, Bitsy?"

Bitsy came out from behind the desk and they hugged. She was holding a little dog, a plump, happy-faced fellow.

"Elizabeth," she said to Jesse. "Well, everyone calls me Bitsy because I'm tiny." They shook hands. She was short, not quite five feet, maybe ninety pounds. "This is Rosie Pig. She's special."

"Piglet," Mars sang. She was a white and brown chihuahua with a round head and thick body.

"Yes, my special little piglet," Bitsy said in a baby voice. She bopped her around in her arms for a bit like a newborn, squelching several kisses on the back of her head. The dog's eyes were half closed, tongue out.

"That dog looks so stoned." Jesse knew inbreeding caused mutations in some designer breeds. Rosie Pig seemed just lucky enough, round head, cute snout: none of her features appeared grotesque.

"So how is everything? I heard about what happened. I'm so stoked to see you!"

"Yeah," Mars said, "It's been crazy, I mean, wait, did you know Jesse..."

"Oh shit, wait, you guys know each other?"

"No, we actually just met over lunch."

"That's so chill," she declared. "And now you're about to blast off," Bitsy teased, gesturing a needle injection into both sides of her head in a brash way.

"Precisely," Jesse said, smirking, brushing a hair out of his face then stuffing his hands into his pockets.

"Seems legit, though," Bitsy went on saying. "That whole thing seemed so gnarly, who even was that shooter? Some kind of Kardashian-obsessed stalker, right?"

Mars shrugged, nodding.

"I don't actually know his name," Jesse said. "I've kept my distance."

"That's chill. Another guy who thinks he's special. So Mars, Marsy, it's been forever! You've been in New York?"

"Yeah, I'm doing the bicoastal thing. I'm back here to do some extra stuff in a pilot that got picked up by NBC. Nothing interesting. What else, I'm doing a shoot this weekend in Venice, too. How are you? How's your sister, how's Rosie Pig's career?" She put a bit of ironic emphasis on the last word.

"Sister is great, of course. Rosie Pig is shining as ever."

"Rosie Pig's a celebrity," Mars explained to Jesse, hinting with her tone. Despite the dog being at Jesse's feet, Bitsy showed Jesse a picture of a piggish-looking chihuahua wearing tiny reindeer antlers, apparently the wallpaper photo on her phone.

"We're taking photos with the public at The Grove Saturday if you want to come. Manny the Frenchie is going to be there."

"Is that another celebrity dog?" Mars asked.

"I thought his name was Marnie," Jesse said.

"No, Marnie is a totally different dog," Bitsy said, sounding impatient. "Harlow and Sage are going to be there. They just signed a book deal. Manny the Frenchie also has a book out. That's our next goal. Then no more temping, no hustling for my SAG card."

"A book deal for a dog?" Jesse asked.

"Last time some three legged Pomeranian soaked up all the attention. I wanted to boot that yappy little bitch outta there by the time the event ended, she thought she was special." Her cackle filled the room. "Hey look what's on!" A flatscreen mounted on the wall was rolling the intro credits to *Retinue*. "So you're engaged?" she pointed to the ring. "To...him!" Bitsy threw her arm out, pointing like a dart as Marc's Greco-Roman beauty bloomed on the screen.

"Yeah."

"He is totally just playing himself, right?"

"Something like that," Mars said. "He's on his way back from a bachelor party in Vegas tonight." Jesse felt sick hearing this. He was sure his face had gone green, if not gray, and he felt he might throw up if the conversation continued.

"It's so ironic he always played this tender sort of background boyfriend in all those movies, and now he plays the star of this sort of clique of douchebags. How long have you even been dating?"

"Six months. He lives here, technically. He's renting a house in Hancock Park, next to what's his name, Pierce Brosnan."

"Who are you shooting for in Venice?" Jesse forced himself to interject.

"Banana Republic. They flew me out." She beamed at him, as something inside him died an uncinematic death.

"Oooh," Bitsy delighted.

"What was the last thing I did before that?" Mars asked herself, looking charmed as she smiled up toward the ceiling to think. "Oh, right, I was a stand-in for Cara Delevingne in um, *Paper Towns?*"

"Cara is so hot, I actually want to hate-watch that," Bitsy said.

"It was only a few shots with a hoodie on, though," Mars said with polite enthusiasm.

Jesse knew all of this of course, from googling her, reading her IMDb credentials. She'd been successful enough to have her entire acting credentials online, her career facts and physical characteristics knowable by potential casting directors in seconds:

Representation:

Ann Wright Representatives, Inc.
Metropolis Artists Agency, Inc.

34

Physical Characteristics:

Gender: Female, Height: 5'9", Weight: 110 lbs., Hair: Brown, Eyes: Hazel/Green
Dress Size: 0, Pant Size: 0, Waist: 24", Hips: 34"
Bust/Chest: 34", Cup Size: B, Body Type: Slim, Sporty
Portrayable Ethnicities: Spanish, Mexican, European, Latin American, American

Experience:

Retinue, Girlfriend, Season 5, Hulu
Mad Men, Waitress, Season 3 (core), AMC
Nashville, Bombshell Dancer (core), ABC
30 Rock, Dutch Cousin/Bridesmaid, NBC
Arthur, Arthur's Drunk Party Girl, Jason Winer
Something Borrowed, Hamptons Club Girl, Luke Greenfield
Eavesdropper, Mary, Los Angeles Complex Theater
Violetta, Amber (Lead), Nicole Zambrano
Hostel, German Disco Girl, Eli Roth
Entourage, Supermodel, HBO
Willow Tree, Music Video Lead, That Noise!
My Love, Music Video Dancer, Justin Timberlake
Aztec Records, Lead, Nicole Zambrano

"You're lucky, you could totally play younger. Marc usually dates young girls anyways, right?"

"Yeah, I don't know," Mars said softly. "So you work here?" She seemed to be jabbing back.

"No, I'm a fucking *temp*! One month assignment. Pray for Rosie's career, guys! Jesse Shore, that's a good name, so you're an actor too?"

"No, I'm trying to break in as a screenwriter."

"You should at least get headshots," she said while handing Mars a receipt to sign. She thwacked her credit card down beside it. Jesse peeked at the name, Marsy-Rose Arenas in raised silver. "You've got a teddy bear doll's type of face, maybe he could do a preventative needle or two, hmm, don't you think Mars?" Jesse held his breath, waiting for her response.

"Yeah, he has the bee-stung lips thing, like Kylie, but more rosebud." Mars reached over and tapped his mouth playfully, studying his facial profile as she signed off on payment.

"Plus he's got this whole green aura thing, don't you think? Like as soon as he came in. I could just, like, see this chartreuse mist, this sort of mildew forest vibe. It's a good thing."

Jesse felt lost. Mars didn't say anything. Her bewilderment rushed into a puzzled facial expression.

"What's Rosie Pig's aura? Light purple I think." Bitsy invited them to agree. Mars and Jesse were staring silently. "I must sound like such a stoner. I've been eating these chocolate-espresso edibles, they taste so good, then I end up super high. Then end up taking Adderall to come down. I've been on ADD medicine since I was a kid." She lowered her voice a bit. "Let me know if you want Adderall. Weed and Adderall...that's, like, my jam. You've got to try it. You really get lost in the corners of your own mind." She began rooting around in her bag for something, out of sight beneath the desk. She popped back up holding Rosie Pig. "Mommy, give me some fillers, lift my jowls! Shorten my snout. Make my ears pointier!" She ventriloquized the dog. Jesse couldn't believe what he was hearing. "Don't you wish dogs could talk? Let's all stare at Rosie and try to communicate."

"Why don't you take our picture over here by this tree?" Mars said, redirecting the conversation while walking to a two seat sofa with a tall indoor parlor palm at its side. "Oh my god, it's fake," she realized.

"Oh my god, I never noticed that! Wow, the tree thinks it's special," Bitsy claimed, then dropped to a whisper, "I watered it."

"Maybe it could get a book deal," Jesse said under his breath as a nurse called them in.

Mars reclined in a chaise in the center of the room while Jesse studied her from the corner.

A nurse came and spread numbing cream on her face and left them as it set.

"She's interesting," Jesse said, about Bitsy.

"She's a wreck. You have no idea. So, a few months ago, her identical-twin sister, Erica, signed this huge deal to shoot all these commercials with Sprint. She plays twins."

"That's cool."

"You don't get it, Erica is doing both parts. They cast her in both roles. Guess they aren't identical after all. Bitsy was so mad, she got really fucked up and cut all her hair off. Meanwhile her sister finally convinced the casting director to hire them both for much lower pay. When she showed up to tell Bitsy the good news, she found her sobbing on the bathroom floor."

"Holy. Shit."

"Right? So Bitsy got Rosie Pig as a consolation. I think she negotiated for her right there down on the cold tiles. I heard she's been getting into some heavy shit, too."

"What does that mean?"

"Everything. Heroin, I guess."

"Amazing," he said, loving the horror story. He briefly wondered if he should offer to take Bitsy's phone number and try to help her, answering her eleventh hour prayers and providing late-night talk therapy.

Big Daddy came in—tall, bloated belly pushing through an open lab coat. It was hard to imagine him doing anything exacting. He smirked when he saw Jesse in the corner. "Okay, Marsy-Rose," he said, leaning in quite close. A nurse did the work. Jesse leaned to see the needles going in; there were so many points of injection. Big Daddy blotted at the sites as the technician kept moving around her face with the needle, injecting willy-nilly.

"I always keep my eyes on the guys," the doctor turned and waved in Jesse's direction. "Sometimes they pass out. Is your boyfriend weak?"

Mars had her eyes closed, and before she could answer the doctor injected near her lip; she seemed to be smiling through the pain. The in-and-out of injecting was endless. He stabbed and stabbed.

"How's mom?" the doctor asked.

"She'd love for me to bring her back," Mars said. Jesse almost laughed. "She always talks about 'Big Daddy' now. My dad hates it."

"A nice lady," Big Daddy said. "Kindergarten teacher, right?"

Mars nodded with her eyelids.

"I treat men all the time," his voice sang. "Bring dad with you next time."

"My mother asked about coming in, too," the nurse said, applying a finishing cream. "I said, 'Ma, we'd have to empty the whole cabinet into your face.'" Big Daddy winked at Jesse, who was breathing again. Mars exhaled herself into the large comfy chair.

"Felt nothing at all, right?" Big Daddy asked.

"Not a thing," Mars said.

Chapter 4: Sacred Pain

Show me your room.

Jesse was lying on his bed, phone balanced in his hands above his face, scrolling. In the days that had passed he had done nothing but breathe. The ground-level doors were open to the pool, a SoCal breeze carrying musty vegetation through The Chateau.

He looked around at something to text her back, but in the context of her request, his décor appeared puerile and stupid. A few Halloween masks were hung on the wall: a vampire face in powder blue felt next to the iconic mask from the *Scream* franchise. He'd painted a crimson accent wall. The only acceptable item was a black paper flower chandelier. He opened the camera and sent a picture.

That's...in your room?

Yeahhh, well Uncle Lee re-gifted it to me. He said it didn't fit the rest of The Chateau.

Wow...your area is the "kids area"?

So sorry you don't like my light!

I like it. What have you been up to since yesterday?

Just laying around.

Wanna hang?

Ohhh.

WANNA HANG?

Haha, yeah! You know I do, okay!

Come pick me up?

Tricky.

?

You just want a ride somewhere?

I want to hangout with youuuuu.

Ok, cool :)

Lee came down, announced by a warning call of Jesse's name. He had a shopping bag and sat down at the edge of the bed waiting for Jesse to pull his attention out from his phone.

Send me your address. You totally can buy me lunch.

Lee took out a how-to book on scriptwriting and handed it to Jesse. Jesse wasn't sure what to say. It was beginner's level, and he felt insulted.

"Did you start with this?"

"No," Lee said matter of factly.

"Oh," Jesse said. "Well, thanks."

"Stories need a scaffolding to drape the themes and emotions and all of that over."

"Makes sense," Jesse scanned the writing exercises and tables as he flipped the pages. Lee was looking around Jesse's room with a curiosity that said he hadn't spent much time down there at all. He was looking over photos Jesse had taped to the wall. He paused over a mask from the 1978 film *Halloween*, which was mounted in a clear display cube and sat on top of a bookshelf. Lee had acquired it as a birthday gift to Jesse a few years ago. He examined it anew as if scrutinizing the costumer's work.

"Prized possession," Jesse said.

"Mmm," Lee mused.

"Do you remember the name of the guy who got it for you?"

The story was someone who worked on the films acquired it from the original set, though without any documentation. Another original mask sold for $1 million.

"I enjoy horror films, in theory, wish I enjoyed watching them." This was a spot of divergence from Lee and Jesse. Jesse loved them.

"Horror is reality. Do you remember the 'Scorpion and the Toad' parable you once told me?"

"Mmhmm? The Scorpion always stings, because he is a scorpion. It's his nature."

"I like the dog and the wolf as an analogy a bit more, because they are two ways of being the same creature, the dog is just defanged. That nature is inside us too."

"The time of the wolf is the raw id," Jesse continued, "like how they say Heathcliff from *Wuthering Heights* is nature, a force majeure. Like, the killer in the horror film, they don't need a face. They're a sense, an impression. And then there's the ego, the final girl, the survival drive, every superhero. We like to watch horror because it resolves these contradictions within ourselves and pacifies us to see the civilized drives winning out. Scorpion nature. Toad resolve."

"Too much downtime is a bad thing for you right now," Lee said, and Jesse saw what had really happened. He'd been given busy work. Lee looked at the movie poster for *Wings of Desire*. "Is this new?"

"No, I've had it a long time."

"Oh."

"You got it for me when I moved in."

"Oh, hmm. So where is this in Jesse Shore's order of things?" He took a good-natured but still mocking tone when saying the last bit.

"I'm not ready to be one of those angels," Jesse said. Lee's eyes softened.

"Jesse, I—"

"They don't participate in the dramas of their own lives," Jesse said. "No mistakes, passions, messes, amends, fights. Being an angel kind of sucks."

"Fun is fine, but that doesn't mean I want to come home and find you drunk in the pool." Lee leaned against a dresser crossing his arms; he looked down at Jesse, who was still laying on the bed. Jesse had his sights drilled into the poster, the solitary angel looking out over Berlin, all alone on the ledge.

"Look," Jesse became irritated, "I know I asked to come back here—"

"And I agreed you should come home. All I'm saying is, there's a lot of emotional fault lines around here." Jesse looked down at the bedspread, picking at lint.

"Yeah," Jesse reached for his phone, hoping there would be something urgent there that might excuse him from the conversation.

"Well, I just wanted to see how you were doing. Don't hide down here all day, okay?"

"Ok, I won't," Jesse said, grateful they ended on a loving chord.

Mars had been staying close by at a friend's house in Silver Lake, though there was no limit to the distance he would have gone to pick her up. He stressed over the idea of meeting a close friend of hers, how those early impressions can matter so much. When he arrived she was standing out front, and they zipped off.

Waiting at a red light, a block out of the neighborhood, he saw something in the passenger door side pocket had attracted her. He recognized it immediately. It was a small, heavy key from the Beverly Hills Hotel, an artifact that had accompanied many infernal occasions and top-down rides around the Hills. She had also found the concomitant bag of drugs.

Jesse blushed as he waited for Mars' reaction. She slowly looked up at him, locking her breath behind a tight-mouthed grin she held in, anticipating his reaction. Jesse thought this look she was making might become a favorite. It indicated she had something irrepressible to express, something sweet or unexpected.

"Jesse Shore!" she boldly overacted.

"You know, it's late, you're a little faded and need to perk up before you drive home, it's life insurance."

"You were probably really proud when you told people that in high school, weren't you?" she zinged.

"Yep." He didn't hide his smile.

She opened the bag and prepared an enterprising bump.

Traffic was blocked past Melrose. Mars loaded the tip of the key again and delicately balanced it as she held it to Jesse.

"I don't actually, well, not anymore."

"Rules?"

"Yeah, no cocaine, no drugs, really."

"No weed?"

"No." At nineteen, he was starting to feel very uncool.

"Anything else?"

"Actually, I don't drink at all. That's my hard boundary." Jesse's breath shortened as he waited for her response. He thought of the bleak history of his substance abuse, choosing among stories from his past while deciding which to disclose in this moment. "I went to rehab the first time when I was fourteen, actually."

"Sexy!" Mars yelled. "Weren't you just texting me about drinking?" She veered to levity.

"No, you were texting me about drinking. I've committed to live gently."

"Right. Actually, what?"

"Well, Lee said I was too young for a twelve-step program. We were at the counseling center, there was a large tree taped to the wall, cut out of construction paper? I don't know. He signed me out."

She was still holding the key up, her other hand cupped beneath it as if it may drip.

"He signed you out of rehab because it was aesthetically offensive?"

Jesse realized now this was true and laughed.

Mars resumed putting lip-gloss on. She mussed her hair in the mirror, closed her eyes, and inhaled until her lungs filled. She held the breath then exhaled just as slowly, eyes still closed. Loose strands of hair fell into her face, sticking to her lips. Jesse had been watching her, and reached over and tucked them back behind her ear. She turned to him before opening her eyes. They held eye contact for a second or two. Jesse didn't know what to do.

"Fuck it. Cocaine is powdered coffee, right?" Jesse surveilled the crowd lined up at a Pink's hot dog stand next to them before inhaling delicately.

"People died so we could feel this way," Mars said. Jesse raced the thought around the track of his mind. All its meanings seemed true. "How'd this get here, anyways? Why this key, what's the story?" Mars dabbed away a spot of powder on Jesse's nose.

"My mom stayed there with some friends as a celebration after her show got picked up."

"What's it called?"

"*Until I See Palm Trees Again.*"

"Oooh, that's so juicy."

"She loved drama."

"Aw, I can tell."

"Yeah..."

"Can we watch it?"

"I don't know, I think Lee may have it somewhere? It's out of production. There might be some used VHSs out there on the internet."

"And do you love it?"

"I've never seen it."

The mechanic estimated another thirty minutes to change the alternator, but after an hour and a half waiting, Jesse and Mars were becoming tired of sitting around, the kinetic energy of their afternoon deflating. Jesse privately monitored the side effects of the drug crash, cautiously breathing slowly as thick clouds silently roared through a perfect blue sky, high above. Mars performed barre using the Miata's trunk for balance, absently staring far away as she talked to her mom on the phone. Jesse inferred Mars was driving the family car, which had broken down, while her sixteen-year-old sister borrowed her own car, a much flashier BMW.

"Who do you think has a higher net worth: Joseph Gordon-Levitt or Shia LaBeouf?"

"Ohhh," Jesse cooed. "Um, Joseph Gordon?"

"Correct," Mars said, looking at her phone. "Okay, what about Jon Hamm or Bryan Cranston?"

"Jon Hamm? He does way more advertising."

"Holy shit, internet says it's a tie."

"How much?"

"Thirty million each."

"Okay, what about, Amy Poehler, Tina Fey and Amy Schumer?" Jesse said.

"That's misogynistic, Jesse, making women compete."

"It is?"

"I'm kidding. Poehler, Fey, Schumer, easy answer."

"Okay, Rihanna, Justin Timberlake and Beyonce?"

Mars thought on it for a few seconds before Jesse interrupted her.

"That one is boring. How about Miley Cyrus versus Justin Bieber?"

"Damn."

"Five...four...three..."

"Bieber, he's got the early Bieber Fever dollars."

"Close, but it's Miley! You blanked on *Hannah Montana*."

"Sorry, hunno," Mars said, sweet-natured.

"Did you see this article, 'Is the naked selfie good for feminism?'"

"I'm listening," Mars said, flipping her hair back.

"'Empowering? Exploitative?'" Jesse read.

"Sure," Mars said.

"'If you tuned in to pop culture last week, you're probably aware of the Kim Kardashian naked selfie saga. To recap briefly: Last Sunday, Kardashian uploaded a photo of herself completely nude (but censored) to her 63.8 million followers. A social media shitstorm ensued, with everyone from Bette Midler to Miley Cyrus weighing in. In response to the backlash, Kardashian later published a post on her blog defending the photo and saying, in part, 'enough is enough [with] the body-shaming and slut-shaming.'"

"Preach," Mars said, dryly amused, while looking at something on her phone.

"'Miley Cyrus, Lady Gaga, Rihanna, and Emily Ratajkowski (to name a few) have all posted essentially nude photos on Instagram at one time or another.'" Jesse mumbled through a few sentences, skipping ahead. "'Is this trend a signifier of female liberation and empowerment—as Kardashian and her supporters claim—or is it just another example of the pressure women feel to display their sexuality and bodies?'"

"In my case, it's a matter of who is in control of the spectacle and why. Yeah, it's probably problematic to post a sexy nude selfie, even if you are 'body-accepting' like Kim says she is. It's obviously on-brand. She shared that pic on 'Women's Day,' right?" Mars put up air quotes.

"Yeah, I think so."

"I don't have a Kardashian body, Rihanna body, a Ratajkowski body. I mean, I don't post nude selfies, at least not for the internet."

Jesse knew this was true from his tour of her photos, though confessing as much would implicate him in the pernicious voyeurism they were discussing.

"It's kind of 'empowering' that Kim posts nudes after giving birth twice. Plus she's a family member, living those roles out in public. That's the beauty of the Kardashian empire, it's a family thing. I mean, they're no Cinderellas. They're just pumpkins. Brandscaped pumpkins! Produced by a team of handlers, make-up artists. I saw this article about this model, what's her name, Tess Holliday, this plus-sized model. It was just so snarky and insincere: 'big news in fashion today,' and 'expect huge things from Tess Holliday.' Totally flippant. The publications know we're sneering through this, like, postured stance towards body acceptance and body reclamation or whatever positive values they're posturing."

"That is cynical," Jesse said, gravely.

"It's not really amusing, like, how does Emily Ratajkowski function when boys jack off to her in that music video, on their parents' computer after school? Also like, why are most of those nudes posted by women of color? That's white supremacy. Where are Taylor Swift's nudes? Kim self-published her nudes in that idiotic book. The one that almost got us killed! When Jennifer Lawrence's nudes were leaked it was called a sex crime. That's patriarchal white supremacy for you. The overvaluation of white bodies. Overvaluing the output of white men most of all. Like, anything you do will be considered more important, more brilliant, brave, more in line with Truth, more worthy, just because you are a straight, white dude."

Jesse felt scolded, looked down and remained quiet. Realizing there was no outside to the pyramid scheme—the wealthy spun the globe on their finger—he puttered around somewhere below. He also had resentments about his own desires; he felt men weren't present, and wielded their wants in volatile ways.

"Well, you should take advantage of your privilege. What are you working on, anyways?" she asked. Jesse wasn't sure how he'd become the focus of this topic.

"Well, I think I'm writing a video game with Marilyn Manson."

"What? Shut the fuck up!"

"Oh, haha, yeah!" Jesse said, much more optimistically. Mars looked into the dark garage. Her car was now up on a hydraulic lift, no workers in sight.

"Let's go," Mars said.

"I told Marc I'd draw the line if he ever got into video games," Mars said, back in the passenger seat of the Miata, "but this seems cool. Marilyn is cool."

"You know him?"

"No, not really, I mean, I've partied with him, Brian. He gave me absinthe. Avril Lavigne was there. I think he was talking on the phone to Lana Del Rey at one point." Mars slid down in the seat, unbuckled, lowered the back rest and relaxed with her arms crossed behind her head. "What's the game even? Don't tell me you just fly around heaven looking for your mother the whole time."

"Actually that's exactly what Kanye West's game is. I think in this one you do that same thing, sort of, but in hell? Maybe you aren't even looking for anyone. You're just trying to survive. Isn't that most games?"

"I guess I just associate games with juvenilia and man-children dreaming of an endless childhood. You have childhood trauma, right? I don't know, maybe this could be an, um, a platform to express that pain?"

The sting of Mars' statement was softened by the surprise that she had learned a bit about his biography.

"Well, both my parents were screenwriters, so it's in my blood. And yeah, I guess a lot of narratives are about some sort of recovery. I guess I'm working on a few things right now."

"Shit," Mars said, rooting around in her bag. "I meant to get my sunglasses back at my car, could we please go back?" She stuck her bottom lip out, flashed her lashes playfully. "Look, I'm putting on my pouty face for you."

Jesse slowed the Miata and looked for a chance to make a U-turn.

"Thank you," she said. "What are we actually doing now, anyway?"

"We could kill time and go see a movie?"

"Mmm...what's playing?"

"We could go to that theater, what's that one called? They do those double features."

"Yeah, sure," Mars said. "Let me see how much time I have. It's four thirty now. Hmm."

Jesse dutifully grabbed the sunglasses, quickly explaining what he was doing to the garage manager, who promised again to give them a call when the car was ready.

When he returned, Mars was on the phone, her tone out of sync with the general frivolity of their day. Jesse looked up directions to the theater while eavesdropping.

"Okay, so, if not tonight then when?" Mars was annoyed. "You sound drunk, it's fine. Love you, bye. Yeah. Tomorrow, yeah."

Jesse turned down Santa Monica, toward La Brea.

"We're still sort of...figuring things out."

They didn't speak for a few moments.

Trucks unloading equipment blocked the entrance to the cinema, though when Mars read the marquee, she squeezed Jesse's arm in delight, bouncing up and down in her seat. They were showing *A Splendor in the Grass* and then *The Sandpiper*. She took a photo with her arms craned out the window like a tourist and posted it.

"I was expecting both versions of *Psycho* or something like that. Have you seen them?"

"Both versions of *Psycho*? Maybe the first one?"

"No, no, *Splendor in the Grass* and *The Sandpiper*?!"

"No, actually! Wait, is *The Sandpiper* with Elizabeth Taylor?"

"Yes!"

"And she's, like, wearing the wife's coat around NYC?"

"No, actually! That's, um, *BUtterfield 8.*"

"Hmm." He felt lost, left behind by her knowledge of film and the speed at which she spoke. His phone buzzed with an amber alert. He hadn't thought to look at it since lunch. Engaging with the screen poked a hole in the good-feeling intimacy of their day. This must be how adult relationships are, he thought. He thought how close to death Mars had come, how they were both lucky to be sitting there now, together in his car. That he had a car. He thought absurdly how he needed an oil change, then looked at Mars while she continued speaking. The fact of their contact at all thickened the lining of his throat.

"*The Sandpiper* takes place in Big Sur. She lives in a birdhouse. You are going to love it: 'A man doesn't love a woman like me, he only…has me,'" she said, doing her best Elizabeth, dialogue heavy on her tongue. She stuffed the decorous hotel key and coke into her bag. "We'll be glad we have it."

The lobby was having its light system redone; machinery lay about, boys from the work crew idled. The bigger obstacle was the clerk at the ticket booth, who'd acknowledged their presence by continuing to read on his phone. He was wearing an earpiece, and when he finally looked back up, he gave them a *why the fuck are you here?* glare.

"Um, two…for both films?" Jesse looked at Mars, who nodded.

"Oh shit, dude, I don't actually work here," the clerk said. "Yeah, we're setting up a film shoot, the theater is actually closed until tomorrow night. I'm just here charging my phone."

"Are you serious?" Mars said to Jesse, rolling her eyes and smiling. "Are those films at least showing tomorrow?"

"What?" He wasn't listening.

"On the fucking marquee?" Her agitation was now taking on an edge.

"It's just for an establishing shot."

"The fuck," she said. Jesse laughed, and then she did, too.

"So tell me what those films are about," Jesse said, as they strolled back to the car.

"Well," she turned towards him, half pivoting as a dancer would, "let's go to that Starbies, then you can see how much I enjoy having a broken heart." She began galloping, then stopped short of his car, freezing in a ballerina's resting pose.

"First position!" she shouted, angling her feet out. "Soubresant!" She leapt. "Arabesque!" She was affecting a French accent with each movement. "Fouetté turn!" She spun. "Fouetté turn!" she shouted again. "Fouetté turn!" She spun a third time, losing her balance. Jesse's palms began to sweat. She lost control and banged into his car, breaking into laughter.

"Mars," Jesse said, stunned by what he'd just seen.

"Okay, sorry," she said, catching her breath, but then quickly returned to a hyper state. "Give her drugs...what's she gonna do next!"

"How about get in the car?" Jesse was almost annoyed.

"Al-right. So *Splendor in the Grass* is directed by Elia Kazan, so there's this whole Russian-Jewish sublimation thing going on," she said as Jesse rounded the car, and then continued when they were both inside. "It's got Natalie Wood and Warren Beatty in it." She took the coke out again and balanced the little bag between her thumb and finger, squeezing it so it puckered open. She scooped the remaining coke out onto the key and snorted it up just as quickly.

"Did you know she's part Puerto Rican?" Jesse asked.

"No, you're wrong! She is definitely part Russian," Mars said, surprising Jesse by dropping the empty bag, littering, really. It blew off into the street. "So, she and Warren Beatty are small town kids. He is the son of a nouveau-riche oil baron, she's middle class. The problem is she can't have sex with him, or anyone really, because 'no nice girl does,' right?" Mars affected a fey vocal lilt to quote the line. "So they're in this suburban environment of shame and cautionary pregnancy tales. It's 1928. He's Yale-bound, this all takes place in Kansas. The repressions all come back as bad health issues. Warren Beatty has his proud-daddy figure that is disgusted that his son doesn't want to go to college."

"So what happens?" Jesse felt apprehended by the spell of her charisma. He admired her hunger for things, to consume her interests with great energy. He wanted her to keep talking.

"There's always gushing water in the transition shots. Natalie Wood has this huge crack up. She's in a tub screaming, 'I'm not spoiled, I'm not spoiled!'" Mars was dramatically overacting. "Then she gets out and delivers this monologue in the nude, to her mom. It's shot from behind, and you can read 'the real' in her mother's eyes because she is the camera in those scenes."

"Damn, so that's how it ends?"

"No, not even close. So she gets better. Finally she tries to fuck Warren Beatty, but he is repulsed by her by now, so she goes and jumps into these rapids."

"Oh my god, she dies?"

"No. She's institutionalized. He goes to Yale. He gets all despondent and drunk, playing solitaire, failing out on purpose. He meets some random chick that works at a pizza place. He doesn't even know what pizza is, haha. So he marries her, Angelina, the pizza girl, and then Natalie Wood meets someone at her asylum and gets boo'd up."

"And then…"

"Then when she gets out of the asylum, she goes straight to see him, Warren Beatty, living with his family on his ranch! He lives on a ranch and has a kid with the pizza girl, his wife, and you see Natalie Wood drive up, with her friends, to see him after all these years, and she meets the wife and…" Mars eyes swelled with tears, "she holds the baby, and she doesn't crack up. And then she leaves, and that's the end."

"I love it already," he said, feeling moved by her unguarded and almost dorky love of the films.

"Actually I forgot the part when Warren Beatty realizes his father is just really a dolt." She grabbed his arm, eyes locked onto his. "So, now, *The Sandpiper* stars Elizabeth Taylor and Richard Burton." Her legs bent childishly under her hips on top of the seat, sitting cross-legged. "It's a morality film, religious codes versus Elizabeth Taylor, icon of the exiled margins!"

"Mars, you're, like, so high right now, oh my god."

"Yeah! So Richard Burton is an Episcopalian minister at this school where her delinquent son gets sent. And he's married to Eve Marie Saint, you know the woman from *North By Northwest*? So they have an affair, but Liz Taylor has this reputation, right? The men are really nasty about her. What's his name is in it, um, Charles Bronson. There's a scene where she throws her own painting into the fire, in front of the buyer."

"When was the last time you watched it?" Jesse asked.

"Oh, ten years ago, easy."

"Ha." Jesse was starting to feel a bit worn down.

"Well, I don't know," Mars corrected, "I guess I found it at a time when I needed it. It gave me this idea, the idea that, what does he say, 'thinking, and living, is a kind of prayer.' Of course, life fell short of everything I expected after that."

"You're, like, the deepest model ever," Jesse said. Mars ran her hand through her hair, beaming a thousand-watt smile at the retort, shaking her head while sticking her middle finger in his face.

"Okay, I was starting to really like you...just don't say that ever again." She was laughing.

He wanted to kiss her; he thought it could be a perfect thing in this moment. He looked down, then away. Mars took his coy gesture as shame. To his delight she reached over and pinched his cheek.

"Hey, I'm kidding," she said, leaning in to look him in the eyes for emphasis.

"Have you seen *V.I.P.*, also with Elizabeth Taylor and Richard Burton?" Jesse asked. "It's about a group of people stuck in the London Heathrow V.I.P. lounge while they're all in an existential crisis. I think about it every time I'm delayed."

"Will add it to the list. Will you order me an 'iced tall skinny almond mocha?' I have to pee."

"Sure," Jesse said, trying to repeat the order back, "Iced tall skinny..."

"...Almond mocha. Pretty sure I'm about to shit my brains out now."

She handed him a twenty and zipped toward the bathroom.

Jesse imagined her sitting on the toilet after peeing while reapplying highlighter or taking selfies. A line had formed outside the locked door. Jesse waited outside, condensation chilling his fingers.

"*Ugh! This weatherrrrrr,*" Mars sang, "the air's all wet from the rain. You can feel the breeze from the beach. You can go back and rot in New York!" She raised her arms, stretching her back. She handed him her drink, ice jostling, and he took a sip. There was lip-gloss on the straw.

Two older men in a work van took notice of Mars; they banged on the roof. "Tushy, tushy, tushy," one said, as the other encouraged him by laughing maniacally.

"One day I am going to stab someone in the neck with a screwdriver," she said.

"Okay Jesse, this is important. What do you see in this picture?" she said, holding the phone in front of his face as they drove back to pick up her car.

"Looks like, um, you're holding a tiny dog in a park. Looks like New York?"

"Yeah, that's my friend's dog, but look behind me, see that guy?"

"Yeah?"

"That's Sean Kennedy."

"Okay, so?"

"Sean Kennedy thinks of himself as this kind of 'fixer.' He makes reality happen on reality TV. He's worked for *Real Housewives of Beverly Hills*, *Basketball Wives*. We kind of had a thing when we were kids."

"Kids."

"Your age, you know." She spoke manically, her hands gesturing wildly. "So he tells me he's running an event for Kim later that day, he's looking for friendly people to be on camera having their books signed, they need footage, he wants my friend and I to be in a shot, so I text him if we go could we cut the line, and so on." She grabbed his shoulder, squeezing hard. "Are you following me? Okay, so I didn't want to go, but I knew my little brother would flip if I brought him a signed book. He likes Kim. So I decided it was worth a try."

She pinched at the screen with her fingers and zoomed in on a different figure.

"See this kid he's talking to?" she asked, turning towards him as she dug her shoulder down to nuzzle into her seat. "That's one of the kids at the book launch. Jesse Shore, listen to me! I think Sean was arranging the whole thing! He hired those protestors. It was all a publicity stunt." Jesse faintly remembered the face of the teenaged boy being held down and cuffed by security. "So I'm guessing he invited these kids to protest. He probably invited the shooter, too."

"Because..."

"Because crazies make good TV, Jesse Shore." An anxiety rushed over Jesse that he'd become taken with a conspiracy theorist, bracing himself for what she might say next. He didn't know Mars at all, and it was possible she'd inadvertently disclosed a spiraling instability. "And since it obviously blew up in their face, they'll have to pay us gobs of cover-up money, lest I expose their gross negligence."

"What do you mean, expose?"

"Sue."

"Oh."

"So," Mars paused, "what's the cost of getting shot?"

"At least a million dollars, two million dollars?"

"No," she paused. "Way more than that."

When Mars' car was ready he dropped her off and they split ways.

Back home, Jesse began typing preliminary notes for his collaboration with Lee, lying on his bed, when she began texting him again.

Bitsy had invited them to crash a party in Echo Park, and the address was around the corner from The Chateau. Jesse checked in with Lee, who was just finishing dinner with Daffy, his sobriety coach and Lee's next-door neighbor, on the back patio. A salad bowl and dinner plates lay abandoned as Lee stood in the pool, leaning against the edge, talking to Daffy. Jesse realized then how serious they both would consider his slip earlier, the bump of coke. They called him over.

"You won't believe what happened earlier," Lee reeled. "I was sitting down doing the crossword in the living room, when two strangers walked through the door, walked right in, wheeling those little suitcases, as one does nowadays. They were renters who had the wrong address, yet found our spare key under the rug as they must have been instructed."

Lee shook his head as he pushed off the side of the pool, treading water as the solar lights began turning on around the perimeter of the property, illuminating vegetation. The familiar squeak of bamboo trunks rubbing together came from the narrow thicket they'd planted as a privacy wall opposite the house. Beyond that, the perpetual lilting hum of the 101 kept going, as always.

Jesse told him his plans for the evening, not asking theirs. Lee reminded him he'd be heading to the hot springs in the morning for a long weekend of R and R. He'd be watching The Chateau, though he was hardly listening; he'd been texting with Mars since the moment they'd been apart.

❖

*You should meet with your agent and tell him
you want him to pitch a reality show about us
haha*

OMG could you imagine!?

What would our celebrity couple name be?

Ohh. Cute question, umm.

You know, like "Brangelina" or "Kimye?"

Thank you for explaining that to me, Jesse

SORRY

Messy

I am, ok. I said sorry!

*No...that's our celeb name:
Mars + Jesse*

Ooooooh Yes!

Hahahaha <3

I'm looking up celeb conspiracy theories...

And?

Plenty of crazy shit

Tell me!

"Did Kris conspire with Kim's executioner?"

Gawdddd

Argument is weak as fuck though

Oh

I could see Angelina Jolie

Why, they aren't enemies?

True

Well...sort of but that's something else
She's got this whole fountain of youth cosmetics line
Competition with the K's

"Kim faked her second pregnancy"
"Kim is the queen of the illuminati"
Oh here is the best one:

"Kris Jenner sold KK's sex tape!"

Those aren't even crazy. I'm looking now.

Mmhmm and?

"Kim exaggerated her pregnancy pains for extra camera time"
^ misogynistic!

"Kim has Kanye under mind control"

Haha! "Did Kris Jenner have Kim's shooter under mind control?"

OMG you're right our lives *would* make great television

"and...we're rolling..."

9:57 Jesse arrives at house, Bitsy is drinking on the porch, holding her dog, entertaining a group of men (Camera A, Camera B, Camera C)

10:01 Jesse sees Mars through window. Bitsy is flashing her bleached teeth at guys she flirts with (A,B) GOOD

10:05 Man in Opening Ceremony tells Bitsy his artwork is very "Whitney ISP" Bitsy says "Never heard of her." (A,B) FUNNY, REVIEW

10:07 Jesse finds Mars at Party. Mars is wearing little white dress, sandals, hair tied up. Glass of white wine (A,B) GOOD

11:00 Man corners Mars. Tells her U.S. is having an "alcohol epidemic." Asks if she wants to go sit down and talk in backyard (A,C) WEIRD, REVIEW

11:03 Jesse flirts with Mars (inaudible) (A) CUTE

11:10 Jesse, Mars and Bitsy walk through the landscaped backyard to a small koi pond (A,B) ESTABLISHING SHOT

11:13 Man introduces himself as "Rich" hits on Bitsy and Mars in front of Jesse. Jesse visibly sulks. "The funny thing about the weather, it's so...up in the air." (A,B) FUNNY, REVIEW

11:15 Man offers to paint Mars' portrait. Bitsy asks if he paints dog portraits. Dog shown eating something in grass (A) AWKWARD, REVIEW

11:20 Bitsy gets yelled at for getting ash in koi pond. Has lost dog (A) RUDE

11:22 Man hits on Mars and calls her "Marcy" (A)

11:25 Sparklers go off in backyard (A) NICE ESTABLISHING SHOT

11:30 Bitsy is very drunk and spills a full glass on carpet. Caterers hand her another full glass (A) TENSE

11:35 Guy sort of dressed like caveman takes them upstairs to do cocaine (A,B) GOOD

11:38 Bitsy goes through bedroom drawers after doing a line (A) FUNNY, REVIEW

11:39 Bitsy finds Hermes Eau d'Orange Verte soap used to scent underwear drawer (A,B) FUNNY

11:40 Bitsy gets a nosebleed and rushes into bathroom (A) SAD

11:42 Homeowner finds them in her room, lets them stay there (A,B) NICE

11:44 Homeowner says she kicked her husband out. Lets Jesse try on his old clothes. Gives Jesse an Armani tuxedo coat that belonged to her ex-husband (B) GOOD

11:45 They descend the stairs. Jesse has the coat on (A,B) GOOD

11:46 Someone is cleaning a wine stain from the floor. Dog throws up something it ate in backyard (A) ESTABLISHING

11:47 Jesse and Mars walk arm in arm out of the house. Bitsy is behind them, texting on her phone, appears lost, drunk, carries dog, etc (A) ESTABLISHING

11:49 Exterior of house

"Look what I found," Bitsy said to them, dangling the bag of coke she'd swiped.

"Oh, nice!" Jesse yelled.

Bitsy was too drunk to drive and would have to leave her car.

"Aaaand...I got this," Bitsy revealed the soap from her bag and smelled it as they walked down the dark sidewalk to their cars.

"Really, guys? I didn't realize I was partying with the Bling Ring," Mars said.

"Oh my god, Marsy. Don't get all judgy on us," she slurred.

"Yeah, so we could go to my place," Jesse deflected. "It's really close actually."

Mars followed Jesse in her car a few blocks to The Chateau, though when he was close enough to see the lights were still on, he balked, not wanting to explain the situation to Lee.

"So, we need a new plan," he said, on the phone with Mars. He had Bitsy in his car with him.

"I thought my uncle would be asleep and we could slip through the back door."

"Oh, okay," Mars said, sounding annoyed. "Let me think, let me think..." Bitsy tapped coke into the nook of her fist and leaned her head down over it, sniffing inaudibly. Jesse watched the half-moon of Mars' face lit up by her phone in his rear view mirror. "We could call it a night, though that sounds terrible because I'm high as a kite and wouldn't know what to do with myself. Second option is to pretend we're all going home and you drop Bitsy off and go somewhere. You don't have a fake ID right? God, is that horrible? I've had a nice reunion with her but I forgot she gets like this, she always needs to be taken care of, just wait another hour."

"Yeah, I don't know," Jesse said, not daring to look at Bitsy in this moment. Mars suggested a trendy restaurant somewhere up on Sunset where they could sit outside and have dessert.

Bitsy was loading up a key again, hunching to avoid the wind snaring around the open top of the Miata, which she'd referred to as tawdry. After several bumps she lowered the sun visor, examined herself in the mirror and groaned. She dug through her bag, pulling out eye drops, which she applied quickly, with impressive precision. She blotted her face with an oil-absorbing sheet then sprayed a floral essence moisturizer. She finished by reapplying lip gloss.

"So," she said, turning toward Jesse while cuddling into the cloth seat, "who is Jesse Shore dating these days?"

He wasn't sure what he was really being asked, but the burn of amour in her glance said the most.

"Well, I've only just gotten back."

"Of course," Bitsy said, "but are you, like, seeing someone in New York? Chatting with people here? What's up?" Her resolve briefly sharpened, and she began coming on stronger, "because I think you're super cute, and Mars already told me you were single, so..."

Jesse felt trapped, not knowing what to say, and kept his hands locked at ten and two on the wheel, his eyes fixed on the road.

"Wait...you totally have a boner for Mars, don't you?" she suddenly hissed. Jesse held his long distance stare with the road, dissociating—Malibu erosion, pharmaceutical ads, a Windows screensaver—feeling Bitsy's ire boring into him.

He'd realized that, like Mars, Bitsy balanced recklessness with a sense of self-awareness hemmed in a wildness that seemed to want out, though Jesse suspected the needs were different in both cases.

"Mars, Marsy-Rose," Bitsy, said, sinking back into her seat, "don't you think it sounds like a bargain store name? She's super obvious too, dating a famous actor, and you know he sleeps with whoever he pleases. I've also heard she's slept with 150 people and that she's much older than she pretends, even older than me, not twenty-five or whatever she says. We should try to look at her ID! Help me distract her? It would explain the lip injections, I wonder how many dicks she's milked with those."

"Bitsy, chill?"

"I'll slap the filler out of her cheeks if she keeps acting special!"

Jesse tapped the brakes to make her miss the bump she'd prepared.

"Hey." She pushed down hard on the back of his head.

He'd learned something akin to meditation during his detours through the mental health industry. To observe his feelings rather than let them intoxicate him, though with all the recent change in his life, he felt far from being at peace.

"I get it," Jesse said, trying to keep cool. "You're frustrated, or drunk and frustrated with, like, your life, or something. And I don't know much about your situation, but anything good could happen to anyone at any time, and a lot of patience goes a long way."

"No," she said softly, sinking into self-pity, "age is a ticking time bomb, it's different for women. The life I want is just never going to happen for me."

The light took forever. He closed his dry, stinging eyes, and took a long deep breath, thinking he needed an ocean of Perrier and more drugs. Ellie Goulding's *Love Me Like You Do* began playing on the stereo, though Bitsy reached over and dialed it down before Jesse could turn it up.

"Okay you're, you're right, you're right, you're right!" she said now, excitedly, taking yet another bump. "I get it, you know, my therapist always tells me the same thing all the time, live the questions, live the questions." She sounded on the edge of tears, her eyes welling up. She reached her hand over to Jesse's nose, and he reluctantly leaned in to snort the offering, but Bitsy lost her balance, spilling some of the powder onto the lapel of his coat.

"God dammit," she shouted dramatically, an odd echo to Mars' earlier impression of Elizabeth Taylor, though now Jesse was getting more *Who's Afraid of Virginia Woolf?*

"Can you just chill for a minute?" he snapped.

A flash went off in a car next to them before the light turned green. Jesse couldn't make out the source, probably a carload of friends having a better time than he was with their Tuesday. A flurry of honks erupted behind him and he lost track of Mars.

GPS indicated they were at their destination, and he saw her car crawling as he caught up, her arm pointing to a spot. He pulled in, turned off the car and put on the club wheel lock.

"I'd be more afraid of having the canvas roof slashed," Bitsy said, fishing a tissue from her purse and wiping her sniffles away, seemingly avoiding a larger fit of tears.

"Hey," she added, grabbing his arm as a lover would tug for a kiss, though she kept a neutral distance. "Let's keep all that bullshit I just said between us."

Percy Faith's orchestral *I Will Follow You* blasted over the empty patio. They'd gone to Melody Fountain, a restaurant offering the easy fun of a roadside burger stand, where vintage pop was piped through the speakers, and you could order a rum and cream soda soft serve or whiskey root beer float.

"Excuse me, it's shot-o-clock," Bitsy whined miserably as a server walked by.

Another customer was moving chairs at a table nearby, looking for something. When they didn't find it, she scoured the area near Jesse, turning up a thin Missoni scarf.

"Jesse...Shore?" she said, leaning in to get a clear look at his face.

"Yeah?" he said, then recognizing her, "Oh, oh my god, Julia?!"

Julia had light blue eyes and long hair. Jesse had hooked up with her maybe once or twice during the hazier years of high school; their tryst seemed ages ago, and she seemed happy to see him, giving him a loud kiss on the cheek.

"Wow, this is slick," she said, rubbing the arm of his new coat. Jesse fondly recalled the details of one of their ménages. He was sixteen, and graduating seniors were having a large afterparty at a classmate's house the night of prom. Jesse was meeting an acquaintance to pick up weed.

The dealer never showed, but as the pool filled with skinny-dipping graduates who'd abandoned their dresses and rented tuxes, he found himself left alone with Julia, who he hardly knew.

"The problem with pool parties is always the party," he'd said, in an attempt to flirt. It was the kind of joke he thought Lee would have made, though the object of his banter hardly responded.

"It's *Day of the Locusts*. But if you joined them no one could see how underdressed you were," she ribbed back at his jab at her choice of social setting. He had on a gray hoodie and popped the lid over his head, smirking.

"No one would recognize me if I steal some of the Waterford, though," he said in the shadow of the hood.

"That's definitely not Waterford," she said, embarrassing him. "Plus they'd know because you were the only one dressed like this," she added, winning the argument. He told her about the pool he preferred, Lee's, and she perked up. Two hours later they were kissing against its wall in the shallow end of it.

Now his focus landed back on Mars, and he knew how badly he had it for her.

"So it's gonna be four?" a server said, handing out menus.

"Why not?" Julia said, sitting down.

Bitsy was texting on her phone, staring into the distance with an agitated look. "Order me a white wine," she said, and they all looked at her, then she got up and went to the bathroom to snort more coke.

"Wait," Julia said, suddenly looking at Mars' hand. "Are you two engaged?"

"He dreams," Bitsy said as she walked away.

Mars had playful concern in her eyes when she glanced over at Jesse, who'd gone white as a star.

"Um, no," Jesse finally said, blushing full tilt.

"Honest mistake. So what has Jesse Shore been up to the past three years?" she asked, with sincere interest. Mars perked up at the chance to hear his autobiographical disclosure.

"Truancy and barely graduating high school," he said. "Moved to New York. Drying out. Then, um, well, did you hear?"

"No, about what?" Julia asked.

"Well," Jesse looked at Mars, feeling responsible for her emotions here as well.

"Oh, god, yeah, I did see that," Julia expressed.

"Suffering together with this one here," Jesse said, nodding to Mars.

"No way? Wait, did you know each other before this?"

"Tragedy brought us together," Mars said. "How do you know each other?"

"Went to school together," Julia said. "I was a year or two ahead, right?"

"I think so," Jesse confirmed. "What's been going on with you?"

"Was just working in the area, stopped in for a drink. Yeah."

"I need a job!" Bitsy piped up. "I'm soooo ready to give up," she bleated.

"What's your job?" Julia asked patiently.

"Temp gigs. Stuffing screeners for guild members. I was a seat filler last month. This month I'm a receptionist. If you have any leads you could pass along I'd take them. If you know anyone casting small dogs!" She hoisted Rosie Pig up, whose body was limp. Her head bobbed melancholically, eyes gone in either direction.

"That's really not my—oh my god," Julia said, recoiling. "What is that?"

"Rosie Pig, she's part dog, part pig. Don't be mean to Rosie Pig," she said, taking a glug of wine, unnecessarily thrusting her pointer finger in everyone's face. Her eyes were red and she was speaking with a manic drawl. Then she answered her phone. "Yeah around the side, outside, do you see us?" She waved at someone.

A handsome guy with long blonde hair wearing a polo shirt approached their table purposefully.

"I'm here for her," he said, leaning over Bitsy, who lay her head back as if she was having her hair washed. They kissed feverishly for a few seconds, tongues lashing like dolphins breaking the surface.

"You wanna get out of here?" she lusted.

"Yeah," he said, coolly. "Nice meeting y'all," he said, leaning in too close with a hand on either of the women's shoulders.

"I'll be in touch," Bitsy sang to Mars as she stood up. She stepped towards Jesse as if to hug him, but instead planted a hand on the wrought iron outdoor table, cupped the back of his head and then kissed him on the mouth.

"Wow," Mars said.

Bitsy slapped the stolen bag of coke down in front of him as if it were a tip for good service before stumbling off after her friend.

"Um," Jesse said, wiping wetness off his lips with his hand. He lowered the bag of coke out of sight, near his lap, then opened it up and tapped the remaining contents to the bottom. Mars handed him the key.

He rotated it so The Beverly Hills Hotel and Bungalows grand hotel font shone in and out of deep shadow and thought of the cruel cluster of promises it must have once represented to his mother. He began feeling upset. He looked down at the coke bag, as if it were cursed, then cleared his mind and took several bumps.

"So what was Jesse like in high school?" Mars asked eagerly, as if he wasn't there.

"Oh, we didn't really hang out much. He was always the brooding, what's the word," Julia was looking at Jesse, "insouciant type. He couldn't be bothered." Mars looked across the table at Jesse fondly.

Jesse knew the years since graduation had been terrible for Julia, having heard rumors about what had happened to her in Florida, though he'd never had the chance to speak to her about it. He knew she'd only been there one semester and moved back, isolating herself in Redondo Beach, and as the tide had changed, socially, he lost connection with her through the handful of mutual friends they might have had.

"So you're living out at the beach? What have you been doing for work?" Jesse asked.

"Well, I had some modeling jobs, some extra stuff, I don't really like the hustle, and I realized it's not for me. And I think I realized I had a miscarriage?" Julia said suddenly, the pitch of her voice rising at the end of the sentence. Jesse glanced at Mars, who was listening ascetically.

"I'm so sorry to hear that," she said.

"No, no, it's okay, I was just talking to my therapist today, revisiting all this shit that happened to me right when I started college, and I realized it happened."

"You didn't know?" Mars asked, softly.

"Well," Julia said, looking at Mars, then at Jesse, "I could just tell you, I mean it's been a while, but I was sexually assaulted the first week of school. I actually moved back because of it, because the trauma was too much. I wasn't leaving my dorm, I was failing out."

Jesse felt a nub of feeling clog his throat. He remembered more of the slur and slander that had surrounded stories about Julia at school, the most popular story going around that she was pregnant and her parents had yanked her out of school.

"All men need to die," Mars said angrily, and very sincerely. Julia laughed.

"Yeah, I mean, I was so green to the whole college thing, I'd heard the stories, but yeah."

"Julia, that's so horrible, I don't know what to say," Jesse said.

"I was living with these other freshmen girls in one of those generic suites in the dorms, and one of them had a boyfriend who lived off campus, an upperclassman who shared a house with a bunch of friends. We all went over there for a party the first weekend after classes started. I remember thinking there weren't very many people there, and the guys were yelling a lot, they had a keg, which was super tacky, but it was almost fun, actually. I remember liking the music. We were all playing drinking games together. One of the guys was taking an interest in me, and I ended up getting really loaded, which was odd because I'd been around drinking a lot and knew my limits, and also I don't really like beer so I wasn't really going for it that hard. The last clear memory I have is finishing a drink and seeing a quarter at the bottom of the empty cup, which I thought was so gross, that I'd mixed up my drink. Everyone wanted to drive over to Miami Beach, but I got sick, and I guess they left me behind with some random guys. So I woke up on a bed, mostly naked, in a room I'd never seen before, and some guy's jacking off onto me, and I think there's cum on my shoulder and in my hair. Maybe someone else is with him, I can't tell. My head was pounding. I threw up again, and that's the end of what I can remember."

"Holy shit," Jesse said, scraping imaginary dust off the table with his fingernail.

"But the kicker is, after getting depressed and anxious and becoming agoraphobic and having my body turn against me, I still hadn't told my parents or anything. I hadn't even confronted my roommate about it. That was the worst part. I mean, you know how it is trying to tell people, they blame you, they don't believe you, anything for it not to be true, right? So I finally told my roommate, and she wasn't having it. By Christmas I was living back home, but things were really weird in the house. I patiently explained it to my parents, who didn't know what to say. They were so proud I was going to the same school as my dad, they even had these totally vanilla lies as to why I moved back that they were always telling people. I think they even started to believe them. They were trying to be supportive, I guess, to give me my space, but I don't know. I used student loan money to move to Redondo Beach and lived off that for almost a year. And, oh god, that girl, my roommate, she actually got married. I saw all these pictures from her wedding. She married that same guy she was dating then. I looked at the groomsmen. I didn't recognize any of them, but even still, I burst into tears."

Julia made a face that made it unclear if she would again. Mars reached across the table and rubbed her shoulder and Julia looked at her appreciatively, keeping her resolve.

"So yeah, I was telling my therapist all of this earlier today, and I realized that one of the reactions my body had was this really intense period a month later. I was having insane cramping and bleeding."

"Ah, yeah," Mars said, frowning.

"And she suggested, well..."

"Yeah," said Mars, who seemed crushed.

Nocturnal fragrances drifted from nearby blooms while patio speakers piddled out nostalgic pop singles.

"I was raped by a really drunk friend when I was twenty, also in college," Mars said after some time passed. "It was a consent thing, he just kept insisting on it. Wow, I guess that was ten years ago."

"I'm sorry," Julia said, tenderly. "And also you really don't look thirty." They all laughed. "Well, here's to us," Julia raised her glass. Mars didn't have a drink but lifted

Bitsy's abandoned Sancerre.

Julia's phone rang and she excused herself to take a call, stepping out to the parking lot.

"She's cool," Mars told Jesse. She was shivering and Jesse gave her his coat, which she wrapped over her shoulders, her legs pulled tight against her feet on the chair. They remained in silence.

"Sorry, trying to give good customer service," Julia said, when she sat back down.

"So, why Redondo Beach?" Jesse asked.

"Well, when I moved back I basically stayed drunk for an entire year, lying in job interviews and taking work wherever. When I got off my shifts, I'd pour wine into Vitamin Water containers and walk the beach, every evening. I never ate. I didn't return calls from my family or anyone. I'd wake up when the buzz wore off, around sunrise, and deal with the anxiety of being alive until I had to go to work, which actually helped. I worked as a waitress. I wasted long days of sunlight as an extra, waiting around on set. Finally I landed this well-paying job as a receptionist at a law firm, but those lawyers were douchebags, always leaning on the high counter of the front desk, where I sat, like a bar, almost, and they'd ask me out, day after day. I couldn't keep friends, and that's when I got into cam work. I'd get drunk and do cam shows for whoever was paying. And they paid, the loyal customers, what seemed like gobs of money. I became addicted. Meanwhile the vultures at work kept asking me out, depleting my emotional resources to politely entertain them all day, so finally I said yes to one of them, the cutest one. He was such a bust, no taste in anything, no idea how to order at a restaurant. I even went home with him. Two words for you: trash dick."

Mars cackled.

"Trash dick?" Jesse asked.

"Dick that doesn't make you any money," Julia explained.

"Oh, I assumed it was dick that didn't give you any pleasure," said Jesse, worried he may fall under these auspices if he was appraised.

"So my drinking got worse, but my career soared. The first day I could afford not to, I skipped work, no call, no show. A week or so later the lawyer who'd taken me out showed up at my door. He must have bribed payroll for my address or something. I sneered at him from behind the curtains with a bottle of Pinot and the best tan of my life."

"Damn," Jesse said, while Mars let out a loud laugh of kinship.

"Men," Julia said proudly, "at least now I can serve them in a way that profits us both. Sometimes I go out with them. Give them the girlfriend experience. Was just with one of them now. We had four hours, but he came in fifteen minutes, so I took a long bath while he read to me. Then we came here where I listened to him talk about repairing his marriage. Anyway, so who are you actually engaged to?"

"My boyfriend, Marc. But proposing was just an embarrassing compromise he made," Mars said, now speaking freely in a way she couldn't have with Jesse. "I'd been considering freezing my eggs, we had a big fight about it, which is funny because I never entertained whether I'd wanted to marry Marc or even have him as the father of my children. I guess he felt like he owed me something because he doesn't want children. A few days later he proposed."

"And you said yes?" Jesse asked, incredulously.

"Oh, child, I've never turned down a marriage proposal," Mars said. Julia laughed. "A week later I surprised him by returning from an out of town shoot a day early, you know, this whole cliché scenario. I caught him with some barely-legal Lily Rose-Depp lookalike who'd spent the night. He was still asleep and she was cooking breakfast in a t-shirt. I invited her to stay so we could all eat together, but she was bugged out, to say the least. So I was feasting on the lavish breakfast she had tried to cook for him when he came downstairs. He was wearing this horrible silk robe that I couldn't stand. He'd stopped wearing it around me because I gave him such a hard time about it. I actually felt bad when I saw him."

"That's horrible," Julia said.

"Nah," Mars said, coolly. "It's his life, too. I never thought monogamy would work with him, he has a wandering eye, it's probably what he's most famous for, other than his acting, which, by the way, is humiliating. He keeps insisting we re-commit, though, which is funny, since I have always been there for that. But we talked things through. Ten years ago I would have felt differently, I would have insisted on the same. He's famous, handsome and has money, and he is in love with that lifestyle, but I guess he has some kind of guilt about it. He even, um," she paused, "about a month ago he paid to get hypnotized because he thought it would help him stop cheating on me."

"Did it work?" Julia asked.

"I never asked," Mars said.

"How long have you been together?"

"Hardly six months. I don't think he's really husband material. We've been having tons of fights. He's away at a bachelor party, doing god knows what. He's been vaguely half-apologizing for the past day or so, sending me coy texts."

"Really?" Jesse said, disdainfully.

"Yeah," she said. "I finally gave him this line I had been saving from when I watched all of *Dynasty*, just to fuck with him, because I knew he was wasted when we were texting: 'What is forgiveness except a way of saying it could've all turned out better, and agreeing to not blame each other for it having not?'"

The night was ending. Julia left, giving them both big hugs before driving off.

"This selfie we took blew up," she said. Jesse had forgotten about it. She angled her phone to show him the numbers.

"How many favs?"

"Just over 10k," she said. "Lots of retweets, which, like, why even would someone, if they don't know us. Always puzzles me."

"Impressive stuff, Arenas," he teased.

"What if I called it off with Marc by posting a picture of my bereft ring finger, wearing nothing but a tan line?" Mars said, rolling into hard laughter, reminding Jesse of an evil Disney queen.

"So, it's really over?" Jesse asked without tact.

"Yeah." They were at her car. She was putting in directions, though her face and posture changed in reaction to something she was reading. "Dammit," she said quietly, smacking her lips.

"What?"

"A nude of Marc is circulating online," she sounded bitter, though far from disbelief.

"Oh shit, that really sucks."

"Yep. And it's not one he sent me, so…"

"So someone hacked his phone?"

Mars glared at Jesse. What didn't he understand?

She shut the door, almost in his face, and pulled off hastily toward the freeway, leaving Jesse alone with himself to overthink the meaning of everything that had happened between them that day.

The phrase "no place to come down" nattered about his head as he approached his own car. He was coming down from the coke high. It had been years since he'd suffered this feeling, and he felt awful. He turned the key half-hoping it might blow up upon ignition to release him from the discomfort of needing more drugs and knowing there were none. He deeply regretted that second haul he'd snorted. And was there a bag buried somewhere in his room? As the Miata turned over, a candied pop song he'd never heard immediately horrified him. He knew he'd ride out a crash easiest without stimulation. He focused on the optical pleasantry of the quick-passing lamplights.

Back at The Chateau, the lights were off for the night. He grabbed a can of seltzer and a plastic container of sweet green olives, then gulped an old peach-flavored THC candy he'd found in the medicine cabinet before stepping out to the pool, to the pleasant-sounding wash of the 101, the familiar frottage of the squeaking bamboo thicket.

He sat on a cushioned chaise monitoring his phone, hoping Mars might get in touch, and as wished, his phone buzzed, though only with an email saying his phone bill was due. He slung it aside, dropping it to the pavement a bit too hard, covering his eyes in the fold of his elbow while taking a deep inhale. He took off his new jacket, admiring the Armani label, then walked to the pool and wet his face and hair, slicking it back as it dripped carelessly down his shirt. A car passing on a residential street blasted Drake, and as his hair dripped down his back, he meditated on the sound of the Canadian rapper that had impacted the party life of the entire country.

His phone buzzed again, and he quickly dried his hands on his t-shirt, then opened an email Mars had just sent with a blank subject line.

I'm coming down and it's fucking uncomfortable.

I know, I'm sorry. Me too.

I'm sitting on my bed drinking ice cold Blueberry Stoli trying to roll a joint. I think I understand your "rules" now.

I've broken all of my goddamn rules today. How do you think Bitsy's night ended?

I really don't care. What are you doing?

Sitting by a pool. Just popped a gummy.

Ooh. So two things: I got a message from organizers of a gun control fundraiser.

And?

They want us to make remarks. Christina Grimmie's family will be there.

Who?

The singer who was shot by that white boy who was obsessed with her.

What do they want us to say? This is kind of creepy.

They want us to appear as survivors and say we support gun control. Super easy.

I think I found it online. Reading about it now. Selena Gomez is giving the keynote?

Mmhmm.

I hope we get paid.

We both get 5k. I want Kim Kardashian to apologize to me on stage.

She's going?

I was kidding.

Oh.

Second thing is a reporter wants a quote from us.

Wait, what? Why?

They are writing a feature, about either this conference or us, maybe both.

About what???

Because we are "survivors" Jesse. Of the gun epidemic. Of pop culture. Who knows.

When do they want to meet?

I'll work it out and let you know.

Kk.

Tell me a story.

???

Tell me a story...

A 19-year-old living off the charity of his uncle has moved from feeling shitty by the pool to feeling shitty in the dark, downstairs level den—furnished in black leather furniture. He is listening to a playlist he made as a teen in order to chill the fuck out while he considers quietly tearing his room apart in search of love and drugs.

You're still a teenager FYI.

Do you feel better?

Ya. Stoli is yum.

Gummy is good.

Are you still wearing the tuxedo jacket?

Nope. I want to repost this picture of us you tweeted earlier?

Sure, as long as you frame it appropriately.

What do you mean?

Write a good caption. Seriously, a *great* caption.

So you're in Marc's house alone?

Yes...that's a weird question.

Sorry, just curious.

Yeah, ok. Had a good day with you, Shore. Goodnight.

xo

♣

In the afterglow of his escalating friendship with Mars, rapt by his own fantasies, he'd been unable to sleep, fighting the persistent nagging stimulation of the coke that was keeping him up. He scraped a bowl for resin, then finally succumbed to taking an Ambien he found among his old possessions. He slept until two p.m. the next day, woke up gritty and hungover for the first time in years, only getting out of bed to go buy medical-strength THC candy bars and a few pre-rolled joints. He pinched the silver wrapper of a weed version knock-off Snickers with his teeth, one hand on the wheel, chewing it as he drove. He stopped at the In-N-Out drive-thru then raced the high home. He spent the afternoon floating on the biggest raft they had, a white swan wide enough to accommodate his cocaine hangover and the paper bag of food, his soul-like essence heimliched out after the twelve-hour rush of attention and emotions; he was stoned and carelessly dropping fries into the blue pool water. He baked frozen mini quiches around twilight, which he ate while watching old episodes of *Lost* on his iPad, the chemical scent of aloe vera gel rising off his red shoulders.

The day hardly happened.

He spent the night working: making notes for potential scenarios and horrifying visions a character may need to face in a figurative psychological hellscape. He was losing himself in description when around eleven p.m. someone rang the doorbell. It was Mars.

"Hey," she said quietly, walking towards him. "Sorry to crash your party, I just..." She stopped there, the answer to a wish he hadn't known he'd made. She had on a knee-length A-line skirt and matching crop top. Her hair was in messy curls; she looked like she hadn't slept. "So this is the house with Echo Park's most valuable pool?"

"Yeah," Jesse said, trying to force himself into the charming character he wanted to play for her.

"Is that her?" she asked, looking at a portrait of Jesse's mother. It was among the first of several photos one saw upon arrival, and therefore one of Jesse's most overlooked. "Very Krystle Carrington."

"Yeah, I guess so," Jesse said proudly.

"Bitsy's car is still out there?" She lingered in the doorway, and then she stared down remorsefully at her plastic sandals, her hair falling over her shadowed face. "Unless you've invited her over." If she was joking, she didn't laugh, and the music she'd carried the day before was absent. "Marc came home this afternoon. He broke down, dumped me, broke off the engagement, so...I just needed something to do besides sitting in a hotel alone crying over room service or drowning myself at a bar."

"What did he even say?" Jesse asked, then quickly added, "Sorry, never mind, I shouldn't have asked."

"What's in your fridge? I'm trying to be responsible and eat something," she said, disappearing into the house. Jesse hurriedly followed her, barefoot in his black and white spotted swimsuit and gray sweatshirt. "And to answer your question, we both knew it wasn't working out. What do you say when it's so obviously over? I wished him well."

They made popcorn and stood on the first floor balcony, looking past the pool to the skyline.

"I was thinking about grace today," Jesse said.

"Like capital 'G' grace? Grace Coddington?" Jesse knew she was taunting him. "Today's grace is my hair being the perfect level of unclean that it will bend exactly to my will without looking overtly dirty."

"No, just like, as a trait, the ability to act gracefully, to be with grace, to think and be graceful with people."

"Grace is a religious concept so, I'm not sure you can have it without."

"I think grace matters most in the absence of certainty. Like, um, conduct in relationships with people?" Jesse regretted the comment, worrying he implicated Mars' boyfriend as a bad person. He wondered if that was his intent.

"Did you realize this on a non-speaking retreat or something?"

"Ouch." He deflected back to her.

"You make me miss New York," she said, pinching his arm. His hands were in his pockets. She grazed from the bowl of popcorn, letting loose pieces drop down wherever on the patio below them. "Grace to me is...," she said, slowing down her words, "I try not to do harm to the people I love." Her tone had become morose. "My anxiety and anger and flight or freeze triggers aren't going away. I guess I try to center myself in a perspective where I think, what can I contribute to this?"

Jesse hadn't thought of it in these particular words, but he found in them a reminder to soften the emotional abrasion he'd defaulted to since the shooting.

"Show me more things in your house," she said then, turning and walking back inside.

Mars *oooh'd* when Jesse showed off a THC Rice Krispie Treat he'd also bought, as large as a bath tile, though much brighter, with neon flakes of blue and green and red. He showed her the house, giving her a tour of their photos, each with their anecdote. Jesse had given himself a similar version of this tour days ago, and the portrait of his mother was equally paused over, which Mars doted over as generously as she had with the confections. He knew the picture well, of course, and had long loved it, its silver sterling frame with an ornamental French ribbon, and the image itself, Patricia before Jesse was conceived, alone at a wedding in a pale blue dress, smiling at some private thought, her eyes cast down, her sandy blonde hair always about to cover her face, a touching, perfect candid photograph.

"She has that type of beauty that gives me a very specific feeling."

"Hmm, what is that?"

"It's the same feeling Joan Collins gives me. That I couldn't exist in the same world as her. If we were in the same place at the same time, let's say we are at a restaurant, and she looks around, fiddles with a piece of sashimi, I am not in her world." She set the picture down. Its image and regal frame cast the Italian-made though also much plainer Tiffany's frame beside it in a minor role. It contained a photo of Lee and Patricia on vacation with friends as teenagers.

"She hated sushi," Jesse said, exaggerating the fact to put down Mars, feeling she was projecting a bit too much onto his mother, assuming a familiarity that stirred resentful jealousy in him.

"You have her forehead, and her nose. They're good proportions, she's got the 106 degree angle," Mars said.

These compliments had been hard to hear for more than a decade, to have his dead mom doted over, though he had heard it hundreds of times, that he looked like her, because to admit that would be to admit the reconciling solution to his grief, that she may live in him, and he must find a way into a future without her.

"Anyway, would you mind if I crashed on a sofa here tonight?" Mars asked, frankly.

"Yeah, that's okay," Jesse said. "Just take my bed, I can sleep on the sofa."

"No, no, I wouldn't do that, seriously, just give me a blanket and I'm fine."

"No, really, it's okay," Jesse pushed. She went in his room and closed the door to change, but after Jesse lay down with a quilt on the sofa, she texted him asking if he wanted to smoke a bowl. *I guess I'm back on weed*, he wrote back. *No parents, no rules.*

He found Mars cross-legged on his bed in a pale pink T-backed camisole and matching drawstring shorts. Not thinking much of it, while waiting to grow tired, he saw she had opened his laptop, and the open tabs told a desultory tale, not that he remembered much of what he'd been doing before he'd passed out the night before in his pharmaceutical haze.

The first tab showed the image of the two of them that he'd scheduled to post this morning. The next was the end of the first episode of *Retinue*. The third tab was search results for Marc Pevier's height, next to that was an image search of Mars, and the last, most recent tab was a porn site.

"Quite a bedtime story you've put together for yourself."

Jesse blushed full tilt, feeling an urge to grab the computer from her hands and throw it in the pool. Instead he stood frozen, not actually sure what he should do.

"Come here," Mars said, scooting over. She clicked on the scene he had been watching, but it had timed out and defaulted to a home page of new uploads. She clicked on the first video. In it an Asian girl in a black corset knelt before a slim forty-ish man. Without comment or any setup the scene began. He tugged his shorts down and pushed his heavy, low hanging cock towards her face. *You know what this is?* she asked him quietly, looking up at him. *A big penis*, he responded impatiently. *No, a fat...mushroom...head*, she said, rubbing her fingers around his large tip. The camera moved in closer as he put his hands on the back of her head and she took one-third, then more than half of him into her mouth, straining to open wide as he looked down at her past his slim, drooping figure. *Suck the cock.* She opened further and began to gag. He moved his hips in closer and pinched her nose, holding her tight in place as she pushed back forcefully against his thighs. Finally he released her head and she shot back, desperately sucking in air, gasping audibly as spit spilled down her chin. After a few seconds she began again.

"*Oriental Desires*, scene six," Mars said. "This is what men want, I guess. To feel like a man. Is that what you want, Jesse?" She sounded angry.

Jesse ran his hands through his hair and exhaled.

"What kink were you searching for, I bet I could find it here..." She moved the cursor and clicked "back" on his tab. "Oh here it is, 'petite brunette,' yeah?"

"Oh, for fuck's sake," Jesse blurted, lunging in to grab the laptop, which she gave up easily.

He stood up and made to walk to the doorway.

"Relax, I'm just playing. Everyone looks at porn, babe, don't you know how to use an incognito browser?" She had stood up when he did and grabbed hard onto his arm. "Petite brunette," she scoffed to herself. She looked down at her body and sway-danced slowly with herself for a few seconds as if celebrating.

Jesse left to process his embarrassment on the couch. The house was quiet, and once the body high took hold, he fell asleep, though after some time he felt a nudge on his shoulder. Mars was standing over him.

"I can't sleep. Maybe, could you just come to the room for a bit?"

Jesse stumbled behind her, rubbing his eyes, shirtless with only short cotton shorts on. He sat on the edge of the bed as she got back under the sheets. She lifted her hand and motioned for him to come towards her. Jesse desperately shook the heavy cloud of sleep from his head.

Mars peeled back the blanket and Jesse lay down beside her, tugging down her shorts. He slid past her waist, and began working through the day's sourness and sweat, her legs lifted over his shoulders.

Mars clutched a handful of Jesse's hair, bracing against a strong orgasm. Jesse moved back beside her and she put her hand on his cheek, directing his mouth towards hers. He braided his fingers through her hair as they made out. She reached for his shorts, seeing what he was up for, and asked if he had a condom. They fucked until she came—it took only a moment, her nails clawing his forearms as she grasped onto him, holding her breath. After she'd finished, she pushed him off of her, lost in her own recovering, catching her breath.

"I realized I wasn't sure how much of this you wanted," she said, between breaths. "I mean I know you wanted it, but that's different than realizing it."

"Oh," Jesse said, "I was pretty close, actually."

His arms were scratched; he'd have marks for days.

Jesse fell asleep so deeply he seemed to begin dreaming immediately. He woke an hour or so later to noise coming from the upstairs living room.

Lights were on, Mars was awake. She'd put music on—*Good Vibrations* started to play loudly over Lee's expensive sound system. The song had never sat right with Jesse, with its cursed timbre and iconic theremin soaring like a feathered demon. The familiar shrill shocks of the introductory notes sounded into the room. A bottle of Maker's was on the coffee table, and Jesse saw Mars bending towards it. A bag of coke with the residue of her preparations was beside it.

"Marsy?" he shouted, using her name this way for the first time, surprising himself with how fully he felt having yelled it. She had changed back into her regular clothes. She didn't respond, so he stepped around the table into her field of vision. When she saw him, she stood up and put her arms around his neck, as if she was going to ask him to dance.

"I'm gonna take off, I promise, just need my phone to charge a little more."

"You're leaving?"

"I want to meet some friends."

"Nothing's open right now," he said. She grimaced, pushing back away from him.

"They're in a hotel, it's a hotel party at The Line, don't worry about me."

"Why don't you just come back to bed?" He cut the music.

"Jesse," Mars said sweetly, easing to normal volume. "I'm just going to meet some girlfriends. Can't you see I'm a mess right now? And I probably will be tomorrow, and for a while after that." She stood and was clearly tipsy. She picked up the bottle and the cap and handed both over to him. She put the drugs into her purse, wiping the table with her hand.

He insisted on waiting with her by the door. She dashed down the driveway the second she saw a car begin to slow, giving Jesse a quick hug as an afterthought, and was gone just as mercilessly as she'd come.

Marc is Moving On!

A recent guest appearance by A-list cutie Marc Pevier may have been a bit awkward: He appeared remotely at a star-studded shindig for a recent convention in support of gun control action, a bill shared with co-star and former fiancée Marsy-Rose Arenas, who plays alongside him in this season of *Retinue*.

Signs signal Pevier has moved on, appearing with an unknown girl in a Las Vegas pool last Friday. The two smooched and shared a fruity drink in the late night hours at a party hosted by Tyga.

Marsy-Rose Arenas appeared here on the arm of Jesse Shore, fellow shooting victim. The two met after surviving a haywire attempt on Kim Kardashian's life during a public event. Asked if the two were an item, Arenas offered no comment. We think Shore's eyes say it all.

Chapter 5: Shooting Stars

The San Jacinto Mountains looked like a screensaver, their musculature frozen in relief, pompous and romantic over the inflated property valuations and Tesla charging stations and poolside hotel services. After a phone consultation with Mars' agent, as part of damage control, Jesse had joined all the same social media platforms she used, normalizing his minor status in the collective imagination of the 15k followers he'd picked up over the past weeks. It was a task of unenjoyed labor.

Once she finished shooting in Venice, Mars had flown back to New York to celebrate a friend's birthday and work a two-day acting gig. Jesse tapped deep reserves of restraint in the week or so they were apart, talking himself out of texting her every few minutes. They developed a daily routine, where they'd have an all-day silence, then Mars would get in contact just after twilight PST, when she'd had a few glasses of wine or was out for drinks with friends, sending him photos and other frivolous updates of her goings-on about town.

When the tabloid stories broke days earlier—*HollywoodTuna* released an article showing Marc kissing Hailee Steinfeld at The Palms—paparazzi came for Mars to dig up anything they could.

She called Jesse, crying and furious, cursing everything from Santa Monica to Long Beach, the Redwoods to Coney Island. By the next day the convention organizers had canceled their appearance in Palm Springs. Mars sounded beaten down when she gave the further bad news over email to Jesse, who desperately needed the money, his last paycheck deposit from New York hardly covering the gas to get out to Palm Springs. Mars pleaded with her contacts at the conference on Jesse's behalf, to no end, though Jesse did some investigative work and saw Selena Gomez had canceled due to bronchitis, her replacement TBA.

"I'm not Selena Gomez," Mars impatiently stated on the phone as Jesse suggested she try to leverage the cancellation, though Jesse quickly backtracked, unwisely suggesting Marc as a celebrity replacement. Mars laughed it off at first, but when Jesse pushed for an answer, she asked him to fuck off. The idea must have stuck, though, and Mars' agent surprised Jesse with the news a few days later that Marc had agreed to do it, and the organizers had agreed to have him.

His heart fell when he realized what he'd set himself up against. He spent several hours in riotous panic at the thought he may have inadvertently brought Mars and Marc back together, but Marc was busy after all, agreeing only to send a video of himself reading a speech. Coming through with Marc was good enough to get them back on the bill.

Asking Lee for money was beyond reason, though he had set him up with a shit-paying job: reading books for a production company, marking their potential for film adaptability as "yes," "maybe" or "no," most of them being "maybe" or "no." He skimmed the novels, and when that got boring, he busied himself with his most personal task: working out the treatment for his show.

A freelancer who was covering the conference for *Politico* had been in touch with Mars in advance of the appearance, and when the images of her and Jesse began circulating, she recalculated her idea, pitching a separate piece altogether to the *New York Times* style section, an article that would require Jesse and Mars to spend time together with the reporter over the weekend to get to know them. Mars promised to take the lead in shaping their impression. For Mars it could be huge; she had several career-making auditions coming up, and suddenly their all-expenses-paid weekend holiday for the Fourth of July was back on.

Jesse had spent the days leading up in leisured activity, jostling between sketching his TV pilot and slacking through his day job. He'd finished his job for Brian, finding the ideas easier since he cared less about them, and when he'd reached a satisfactory end point he'd sent along the script to Lee, nervously refreshing his email waiting for that response to arrive.

"It won't blind any queens," Lee said on the phone to Jesse, who was barefoot on his balcony at the Riviera Palm Springs.

"Is it workable?" Jesse asked sadly, cutting to it through the unexpected sting of his response.

"I'm not sure," Lee said, on speakerphone in the backyard at The Chateau. Jesse imagined him filing his nails on a chaise or leaning on the edge of the pool in his usual spot. "Maybe, yes," Lee shouted through the phone.

"Okay, so what's next?" Jesse asked as he considered panicking.

"I'll touch it up and pass it along." Lee sighed. "But Jesse, I need to tell you something. I've declined the project, personally. Brian says he understands, but I believe he's angry. You know people in Hollywood, they don't like to hear 'no.' Anyway, I think this has become a bake-off—I've heard a few other people are working on a script. Don't get your hopes up."

"Well, I've got some other things going on now," Jesse said.

"Yes, I hope you've been enjoying the day-job or whatever it's called nowadays," Lee said.

"I have, actually," Jesse said.

"Because it's harder to get you a shitty job than it is a good one, somehow," Lee said.

"So get me a good job," Jesse said, testing his confidence.

"Bravo!" Lee yelled again. "All in time. Good luck later, and remember less is more, always. Trust no critic," Lee said. "And how's your sobriety through all this?" He put pressure on the word.

"She's not a critic. She's a reporter," Jesse said, suddenly put on the defensive, slipping the question entirely.

"I'm so sorry to hear that," Lee said.

Jesse knew Mars had arrived before him, and knowing she was on the grounds sent interludes of violent nerves upon him: he scanned for her in the parking lot, then in the lobby, peeking into the adjacent restaurant, and again lounging poolside as he walked to find his room, not seeing her anywhere, and when he called she didn't answer. Finally, she texted him back: she was in the spa getting a cactus body wrap and subsequent sugar scrub. He wanted nothing more than some down time with her, but when she said a car would be waiting for them at four thirty, asking to meet then, he disappointedly began lint-rolling his outfit for the evening.

Mars was late, appearing with big curls in a stunning Dior black knee-length dress, looking more Met Gala than charity event, attracting the attention of several men waiting in the lobby as she breezed through, kissing Jesse on the cheek to say hello. Their call time was moments away. They rushed into the car, Jesse wearing a black blazer with a white t-shirt over black jeans, but the driver wasn't theirs, and it seemed there'd been a clerical error by one of their handlers.

Jesse pulled his Miata around while Mars dialed up directions to the JW Marriott. "Don't lock your knees," Mars said, as they zipped through the desert, Jesse driving recklessly oblivious to speed limits and his surroundings, accelerating too quickly and braking uncomfortably hard. "It's the first thing any actor needs to know, especially if you're standing around a long time. Jesus, Jesse," Mars said, bracing herself against her side of the dashboard as he halted before a red light.

"Will we be?" Jesse asked, expecting only to read the short speech off of a teleprompter he had practiced reading earlier this week.

"Maybe on stage, not sure," Mars said. "Actually we may be seated for the dinner, probably at a table up front with the other guests."

Jesse's nervousness battled the intoxicating high of finally being with her again. Kesha blasted through the stereo as Mars rushed to post an image from her phone of herself holding a detox tea by a company sponsoring her.

"Does that stuff work?" Jesse asked, one eye on the photo as he drove.

"It's green tea with senna," she said, "I drank it once and shit my brains out." Mars then began streaming live to her feed of followers, panning across the sky, then onto the conference center and event signage, which was quickly coming into view. She panned to Jesse, who felt affronted and waved awkwardly. He nearly missed the turn into the hotel and carelessly smashed the brakes. A close-following SUV struck them from behind.

"Oh my god. Oh my god," Mars screamed. Her live video kept streaming as the phone careened down against the floor mat.

They were fine, of course, though a bearded man in a t-shirt and shorts impatiently stepped down from the vehicle behind them.

"What the fuck was that?" he asked as he checked the front bumper of his GNC Terrain, which was hardly damaged, before noticing the smashed rear end of Jesse's Miata.

"I guess we should get out of the road," Jesse reasoned.

"No, we need to get into that hotel," Mars said desperately, getting out of the car. She was holding her phone, still recording.

"Wait, you're Judd Apatow?" Jesse couldn't believe his luck. Mars put her phone away.

"Yeah, that's the name on my insurance, so if you don't mind—"

"We don't mind. It's just...we really have to go. We're late. Come on, Jesse." She pulled a scrap from her clutch for them to exchange information. "Let's have lunch tomorrow as additional compensation for this."

"No chance," Judd turned to Jesse, then Mars. "I'm throwing out the first pitch at Citi Field tomorrow night." He looked at the Miata, whose engine was choking in starts and fits to keep turning over, its rear bumper sagging, exposing some of the metal frame. "You're not...scientologists?"

"No. Definitely not," Mars said.

"We have a lot at stake in there," Jesse said to him, getting angry.

"Oh, this is part of Angelina's thing that's happening this weekend."

"Yeah, exactly," Jesse said, not knowing she was involved.

"Well, whatever," he said, scanning over the hotel and conference center for proof as to who they really were.

Jesse tried to get the car into the lot, though it scraped to a halt just as they'd pulled past the signage for the conference, not far from where the accident had just taken place. They trotted the long stretch towards the hotel beneath dusty susurrations of pale orange sky.

"Lunch? What was that about?" Jesse asked.

"You got his number too, right?"

"Oh, um, no, actually."

"Dammit," Mars said, walking ahead in frustration. "You need to pitch your show to him. I was trying to get you a meeting."

"I think he's gonna call," Jesse said, following her. "He said he would."

"He definitely won't."

"Give them space!" their handler shouted as they settled into the green room.

Trisha, a cute Asian twenty-something who seemed just out of a goth phase, had been assigned to the less-important speakers, and had inserted herself between them and the camera crew documenting the conference's backstage activity. An older woman in a suit—apparently dissatisfied that miscreants were still on the program—looked at them discouragingly just as her phone rang. She recalculated her visage and answered with a warm greeting.

"Hello?" she sang. "Murphy's finally arrived? Wonderful..."

She meant Senator Chris Murphy, who was scheduled to deliver opening remarks; Mars and Jesse were on after that. Their speeches had been woven together, and they'd simply need to read the color-coded phrases from the teleprompter—"same as you've seen in advance, no big deal," Trisha said as Jesse's chest surged with nerves.

"You think I can stand up on stage next to her?" he said to her, as powder was reapplied to Mars' face to absorb the sweat from their dash.

"I think you are going to do your best," the handler said, giving him a hard time before giving way to a friendly laugh. "I need you to sign these releases for the film crew. All of this stuff was on the contract we emailed you, but I wanted to give you some time to chill before getting you on film. They're shooting a virtual reality story feature for *The Nation* on gun violence. There are several reporters here, too, just sort of around, talking to people. Try to be patient with them." She squatted down between where they sat and began speaking more intimately. "I never cared about the 'drugs' thing, by the way. Those decisions come from the planning committee. So seriously," her friendliness calmed Jesse's nerves, "if you need something just let me know." She swept her bangs out of her face, looking him over, then picked a spot of something off of Jesse's collar. She seemed to be in control of two interns, both dressed like prep school boys. "Can you ask for another catering tray here? Tell them we need more spring rolls and the crab cakes with the aioli. And bring a few bottles of Perrier."

Across the room, a handsome black guy sitting beside a Kennedy-esque blond, maybe his boyfriend, was giving an interview on a sofa.

"Look, if you are asking me to say 'Black Lives Matter,' I can, easily. But that's not why I'm here, right?" he said. The interviewer said something Jesse couldn't hear, making a note. Jesse scanned the room: besides the sofa, it contained a few generic round tables littered with abandoned paper plates. Handbags hung from the chairs. Skylights above framed the dramatic end of the sunset. Instrument cases were piled in the back of the room. Out on the convention floor a band was playing Adele's *Rolling in the Deep*. Maybe it even was Adele.

"I mean, I think the lowest common denominator in most of these is male libidinal anger though, right? And their inability to bend the world to their will. They always think they deserve that." The reporter made more notes while scanning the room, pausing when she saw Mars and Jesse before turning back to her subjects.

"Those must be the Kardashian kids," the blond boy said, hailing them through the chaotic green room via the pithy remark and a wave.

"Adrian," one of them yelled, introducing himself.

"Robin," waved the blonde.

Savannah, the journalist who they'd be hanging out with, was tall and pretty, with a disarming *Annie Hall* fashion that probably helped get the most out of her interviewees. She leapfrogged introduction into business, leaning in toward Mars. "So let's meet tomorrow, at the..." She flipped through her legal pad. "Riviera, is it?"

"Sure," Mars said, before Jesse could respond. "I'll tell them I have someone coming. What time?"

"I'll pop over there when the convention breaks for lunch? And then maybe we can do dinner? If that's no good I could stick around Sunday."

"Dinner sounds perfect," Mars said, turning to Jesse with a look that didn't leave things open for discussion.

"Two minutes," someone shouted from the door, gripping a clipboard in one hand and holding up two fingers with the other.

"Shit," Jesse said, an involuntary reaction, brushing his pants of invisible grime. Mars walked steadily next to him as they were led down the hall through a door to the side of the stage, just out of sight of the audience.

"Here we go, babe," Mars looked at Jesse, threading her arm through his as a voice over the intercom introduced them to the crowd of nearly six hundred. It was impossible to see anything beyond the footlights. It was almost as if they'd won an award. Mars read the first line, and by the time he remembered to breathe, it was over. The ballroom rolled into applause. Senator Murphy shook both of their hands as they exited. Committee members thanked them as they walked down the hall.

Trisha brought them back to the green room, where she had a bottle of champagne waiting for them.

"I stole this from catering. Like actually stole it from the fridge," Trisha said, scurrying past them with a tote bag—the exact kind that was being used for gifts. Jesse unwrapped the plastic unceremoniously. Adrian and Robin watched from a sofa, then stood up eagerly, as if they'd been waiting for this reprieve themselves. Jesse turned to pop the cork away from them, though ended up with the bottle in Trisha's face. She quickly put her palm over it. "Now you're pushing it," she had an incredulous look. Mars took the bottle from Jesse's hands and popped it into an upper corner of the room.

"What are we toasting to?" Jesse asked, watching the bubbles rise. He held his glass up to the light. *Unreal potion*, Jesse thought, enjoying the phrase. He set the glass aside.

"Marc Pevier's face," Adrian sassed. A small monitor Jesse hadn't noticed earlier was showing a simulcast of the presentations, and Marc's video had just started. "Can we unmute this?"

"Sure," Trisha said. Jesse felt tension while Mars stared hawkishly at the screen. Between the blue of his eyes, his dark curly hair, and the clever bow of his lips, he was more pretty than handsome, as if dreamt out of precious stone, and they all watched as his beauty filled the screen.

"He looks like a hard dog to keep on the porch," Robin said.

"I know everything, so," Trisha confessed, turning anxiously to Mars. "I mean, it's my job to."

Jesse set his glass on a nearby table, feeling relieved.

"It's fine," Mars said coolly. "Excuse me, I'm sorry." As she walked out, she straight-armed the TV, hitting Marc's face, knocking the screen back against the wall. The image scrambled, then froze. Adrian gasped silently and the rest of them remained silent out of respect and adoration. Jesse felt himself falling in love all over again.

They were driven to their hotel in an Escalade. Mars whined of a headache and dehydration, blaming the bodywork she'd had done earlier, and she let her small frame sink into the leather seat, her arm raised with her wrist draped over her face, and sat in silence. It was a sympathetic posture that he could imagine viewing as a classical oil painting in The Met—he suspected she was posing, but she was indifferent to his presence as he continued staring at her frown, the rest of her face now tucked into the crook of her arm. *There are things you can't get anywhere,* Jesse thought, recalling a line from *Holmby Hills, but we dream they can be found in other people.* As she lay across from him, he wondered if she contained all the things he dreamed she might, but in an attempt to divine a truth, as she lay slack in a heap of chenille and Italian wool, all his second sight could see was "Marc Jacobs."

Standing on his balcony alone, Jesse scanned the darkened poolside, where small populations clustered in the open air. Couples in the hot tub nursed their private pleasures. He didn't know which room Mars was in and idly scanned the backlit curtains and half-filled railings that ran the property, imagining her cervine and emotionally exhausted, seated before a vanity, removing her makeup. He checked his phone for messages but had none. His car was probably totaled. For the first time since being back, he missed the uncomplicated loneliness of New York, how over summer he'd settled into a livable routine of labor and leisure. He'd wanted less there.

He had been paid an appearance fee of $5,000. It was the most he'd ever been given for anything. It would afford him to get set up back in New York, or secure his own apartment back in California, should he want that. Maybe he'd move to Tokyo. He future-tripped on the prospect—leaving it all behind.

He flipped through the spa menu and called the desk to order a back massage— the least expensive treatment, not that he was paying—but services were over for the night. He looked at his check again, the ripple of the holographic watermark, standing with his back pressed against the dividers between the room and the balcony, wasting AC, giving himself a little massage against the edges of his spine.

He decided then, finally, to call his father. He stepped fully onto the balcony and made the call. His father answered on the third ring.

"Jesse, hello? Is this Jesse?" It was hard to hear.

"Dad? Yeah it's Jesse."

There was muffled talking, then: "Listen, I'm really glad you called. I'm about to take off and they're making me shut my phone off."

Jesse realized his naiveté and selfishness in assuming his father had been waiting around for his call this year.

"Where are you going?" he asked.

"LaGuardia, to New York, Cher and I. I'm taking off from Chicago. I'm living there now." Many questions emerged. "I'll call you back as soon as we land in a few hours."

Music blasted from the Friday night pool party. His hotel had the cold discomforting staging of a luxury interior photo. Without the excitement of Mars' company, he was by himself in a strange place. He wished he was back home, at The Chateau, and if not home then at a quieter resort, Desert Hot Springs, or the Joshua Tree high desert, a cabin on Big Bear.

His phone buzzed an alert that it was eleven p.m.: time to post an image on each of his feeds. He took a picture of the pool and uploaded it, writing a lazy caption thanking the convention organizers, faking some "well-deserved" Friday evening relaxation. He'd almost convinced himself of his own authenticity by the time he lay on the bed in darkness, now scrolling through everything Mars had posted that day. There was a new picture of her wearing a green facial mask, uploaded from across the hotel grounds, everything but her lips and eyes covered in slime. He focused on her mouth, and his attention displaced onto an abstract yet immediate wanting. He forced his mind elsewhere from the rejection in lying down alone, when it could have been another way, though his thoughts jolted absurdly to the defamiliarized sound of his father's voice, and his anxiousness renewed. He stood up, regretting his decision to call, then ate a marijuana edible before going back out to the balcony again for air. He felt suddenly very alone.

A Kanye song blasted, something old, maybe *Paranoid* or *RoboCop* or *Devil in a New Dress*. Then he saw Adrian and Robin flagging him with huge arm waves from a large hot tub. He went down with trepidation.

They were sipping drinks that had mint leaves as garnish; Adrian was submerged down to his chest while Robin sat on the edge with his shins dipped in.

A European couple that seemed to be giving each other mutual massages soaked in the opposite corner, ignoring the loud conversation from two younger boys, who were doing enough talking for the rest of them. A server came by and Robin signaled for another round of drinks, pointing at Jesse as if to ask if he wanted one. In the shadows Jesse froze up, though Robin asked for three despite his non-answer.

The two young boys had lost a pack of cigarettes among their belongings and were making it everyone's crisis. One of them was an astonishingly toned nineteen-year-old Adonis. And probably an actor. Jesse imagined him wasting his youth on daily cardio, two hundred crunches and pushups a day. His buddy was slobbish by comparison, forty pounds heavier at the same age and height, wearing a Palos Verdes football t-shirt and headphones around his neck. Chairs had been dragged to the edge of the tub where they both sat down. Jesse scanned the perimeter of the property, not seeing Mars, pushing his hair out of his face as the wind blew.

"Get the vial," the chubby one demanded to his svelte buddy, who, to everyone's surprise, produced a small glass cylinder. "Don't you think coke smells like chlorine?" he then said, unscrewing the lid then dipping the tip of his cigarette down inside. Jesse watched them like a movie, a comedy film on a flight the person next to you is watching, his inner monologue reminding him that the responsible thing to do would be order a hot meal to his room, take a long shower and get a restful night's sleep.

"No, it smells like formaldehyde...on my balls," the very attractive one said, embarrassingly loud, though the couple who had been cuddling had since left, and Adrian and Robin seemed entertained by the annoying pair. The boys exchanged the coke, but one of them let it slip through their fingers, and they all watched as it clinked on the concrete, and then rolled out of reach, into the hot tub.

"You stupid, stupid motherfucker," one of them said, before the other landed a playful, low-volume punch back on his shoulder.

Robin fished around beneath the bubbles with his foot, eventually pulling out the red glass vial. He held it up as much in the light as he could. The top was missing and there was nothing inside. The boys had no response, and there was a moment of silence as they regarded the gurgling water as if it had undergone an alchemical transformation.

"So what do you boys do, anyways?" Adrian finally asked.

"I'm Blake," the handsome one said, "and my former friend who just spilled our drugs is Sharkey." He nodded to his friend who raised him arms like a religious figure.

"Blake's playing a lifeguard on a Disney show that's shooting right now. And that's all we can say. Because we're both under contract."

"So what do you do?" Adrian asked.

"I help him play lifeguard: keep him high, keep him alive, and sweep up his scraps." They lazily, proudly, high fived.

Sharkey sipped from an oversized fountain soda from Jack in the Box. He tried handing it to Blake, who declined. He popped the lid and began chewing ice.

"I helped design lighting for a few *True Blood* episodes," Adrian said.

"You've seen that?" Blake asked Sharkey, who was now underhand-tossing the frozen cubes into an empty corner of the hot tub.

"Nah. I mean, yeah, well, I used to watch it with Elisa, but I think we always ended up pausing it to bang, so no, not really."

"Bro, I thought you only hooked up with her a few times?"

"I know man, that's what I'm saying, now it's too painful to try to watch."

"Robin's an actor," Adrian said. "He's a regular on a show called *Poldark*."

"It's a PBS Masterpiece show, like *Downton*," Robin said, speaking more to Jesse.

"Don't know about that," Sharkey said skeptically, and they all laughed, even Jesse.

"You're an actor, do you know who the chick is that's staying next to me, up in room 27? I think she's an American Apparel model, haha."

Jesse felt himself go red, and noticed Adrian watching him while Robin smirked at the teenager's crude libidinal energy.

"Don't think I'd know her. 'Chicks' aren't really my thing, you know?"

"Well, if you do know her," Sharkey said, "tell her my boy wants to meet her."

"Saw her on the balcony this afternoon," Blake said. "Almost had to jerk it right there. Thought it was Kendall Jenner for a minute. Hotter though. She has that big pout-mouth, you know, the kind that looks like a pussy, all wet and shiny."

Jesse was seething.

"What was that other thing you said about it? It was perfect," Sharkey said. "Oh yeah. You would lick her asshole...'til it shines bright...like a diamond."

"Like the Rihanna song," Blake needlessly explained. "Yeah, I used to have her ad taped to my wall. She's down on all fours in this animal skin rug. And it says something in French over it. It's like, *Après Ski*. Something like that."

Jesse's mind unwillingly went to a memory of a leaked cell phone video he'd seen of the head of a cool apparel brand dancing nude to *Naïve Melody* while talking on a phone beside some female employees. Behind him was the bed in the company loft that appeared in the company's signature ads. His cock flapped as he shook his skinny hips. He had a startling, completely full pubis growth. Scandals piled and he was ousted from the company, which he'd started in his bedroom and had continued running as if he was still in that unchecked space.

"Yeah, we got it," Adrian said, looking nervously at Jesse now. "Be careful, you might be insulting Jesse's ladyfriend."

"That's your girlfriend?" Jesse thought he was about to win favor. He was wrong. "But there are always tons of hot chicks to pick up here, man. Why'd you go bringing sand to the beach!"

A phone rang—Blake's, but Sharkey answered it, and indicated, through charades, that they urgently needed to go.

The jets cycled off as the three of them were left alone.

"So where is your girlfriend, anyways?" Robin asked, as if any of what had just happened hadn't.

"Come on, let's chill in this shitty teenage coke water," Adrian said as consolation for the poor company. Jesse let the heat shudder through his body as he eased into the tub. A tray of drinks appeared; Robin distributed them.

"The thing about a jackass like that," Adrian said, sipping his drink besides Robin in the hot tub, "is that in a few years he'll be more handsome, rich, even more famous, with better suited friends, and will be fucking whomever he pleases."

"Just not Kelly Ripa," Robin said, and they both laughed at what must have been an inside joke.

"What's that?" Jesse asked.

"You know, Bieber said he wanted to fuck Kelly Ripa. She said it was a cry for help." They both laughed again even harder.

"And then he ended up with Kourtney Kardashian!" Adrian shouted.

"Wait, really?" Robin asked.

"Yeah, girl," Adrian said.

"Was that before or after the Bora Bora pics leaked?" Jesse broke in.

"After," Adrian said, deliciously, imagining what Jesse was imagining.

"He's so hot," Adrian said.

"He's got dirtyyyyy dick." Robin was now performing.

"Who's your favorite Kardashian?" Adrian asked Jesse, his mouth trying to find his straw.

"Kourtney...I guess. Totally over them," Jesse said, genuinely unable to build up enthusiasm for any of them.

"Oh, right," Adrian apologized.

"No, it's cool. Actually, do you want to hear a sinister conspiracy theory?"

"Sure, queen."

Jesse tried to explain it all. Adrian and Robin were unconvinced, then Jesse asked if he should file a suit.

"Well, this is America. Anyone can sue. But that sounds flimsy as fuck, and even if it were true, that the protest was staged, that happens all the time. I mean, they were filming a TV show? Next time you watch the Oscars, look at the elite sea of rich, happy people. Our issues are not their issues. A-list, B-list even, they're like a second Illuminati, living beneath a protective plastic canopy that keeps our shit out of their hair. Their world's not ours to know."

"Yeah," Jesse admitted, meditating on this. Did he remember waivers being handed out far up ahead of him to people in line?

"And you'd have a hell of a time proving it was connected to the shooting. And even if the protestors were actors, that's not what landed you in this hot tub."

Jesse felt deflated, and wondered why he went along with Mars' theory in the first place. Was she paranoid? He began feeling defensive, but dwelled on Adrian's last comment. "Not ours to know," Jesse said aloud, looking at Adrian now, who also seemed to have taken his own thoughts inward. Robin stared far away.

"Drink?" Adrian suggested. Robin slurped out of the water and they went to the side of the bar that opened toward the pool.

It seemed like a theological question, what isn't ours to know. He'd held a visual representation of his mother's spirit as somewhere else. A distant place where desire suffered no active conflict. A meta-divine realm where spirits wisped their dramas. Belief in Heaven meant a metaphysical order, submission to a higher power to win favor and good fortune. He suffered a block when trying to think beyond this, always talking himself out of "God," though a new exercise now came to mind; what was his consciousness before birth? He'd heard the phrase "eternal oblivion" and thought it was needlessly pessimistic, preferring to think of a pre-birth condition of peaceful resting, which seemed a hard fact he couldn't argue against. But now he knew life; he knew the drama of the cosmos, stars scattered like sand on the shores of some unknown reality, rocks and cells, his self-consciousness an odd tick in time. And when his "I" was snuffed out like a candle, forever, what then—? He closed his eyes and tried to meditate on the imagined calm, all that would one day go on without him.

The other teens, the images of Mars' ads, the limp disclosure of his conspiracy theory, and the general foolishness of being out in the desert alone and broken-hearted, it was all too much.

Mars was blowing him off. His father wouldn't even give him time for a call. He considered simply going back to his hotel room, but knew he wouldn't sleep.

The boys were back.

"Jesse, you're ignoring your drink," Robin teased. Fuck it. He picked up the drink and gulped, taking some ice cubes down as well. He took a second steadier gulp, feeling the immediate burn down his throat. He exhaled as his mental clarity blurred.

"I just wanted to leverage the theory to get this show I'm writing onto the air."

"Oooh," Robin sang cartoonishly. "We're writing a show, too! It's called..." He paused and looked at Adrian. "Brads," they said in unison.

"It's about two roommates who are trying to break into the industry. They pitch a new show every week. That's the gimmick," Robin said.

"And they're both named 'Brad,'" Adrian added.

"Naturally," Jesse said, getting into their performed camaraderie. If he was breaking his sobriety, he didn't want it to be lost on a foul mood.

A Rihanna single came on. It wasn't *Diamonds*, mercifully, but instead a slow song about kissing; cruel and sweet. Jesse reclined, wishing he had someone to make out with, and again the person who had preoccupied his mind so much recently came to mind, how he'd constantly picked apart their short history, their circumstances. It was a tiring practice.

"I should stop after this one," Robin said, stabbing ice with his straw. "I was so fucking hungover today. God," he said, his face lighting up with an actors' wattage. He stood on the concrete deck half-illuminated as his trunks dripped down over his feet.

"What did you do last night?" Jesse asked, innocently. The cold drink was working a familiar magic, and he already thought of how to get another. He was disappointed to hear their night would be cut short. He drained his drink and craned his neck to hail the server.

"*She* got tits-wasted at The Parker. I tried to hang with her but I lost him to the hands of a beefy Mallorcan prince. I was pretty loaded myself, but I get a phone call from this one an hour later asking which hotel we're staying at."

"Ughhh," Robin muttered, as if the painful hangover had reinstated itself.

"What even happened over there?" Adrian asked in disbelief.

"Funny story," Robin said charmingly. "We went to his room. I think he realized how drunk I was and had second thoughts?"

"So he kicked you out?" Adrian asked.

"No, I think he tried to blow me but I fell down, or maybe then I was blowing him. Worst thing is I only went to bed with him because I wanted to know what his cock looked like."

"And?" Adrian arched his eyebrows.

"I don't remember."

Adrian roared and Jesse laughed.

"All I remember is him standing there in a green robe, his awful feet taking up half the room. They were utterly repellent."

A group of friends hovering around a bald man set up across the hot tub.

"Who is that guy?" Jesse whispered, leaning into Adrian, as he watched them pass an impressive joint around, minding the water.

"Mmm, not sure, looks like the guy from *Breaking Bad*, the guy who played Hank? Anyways," he turned back to Robin, "you're going to have to give up these sex-capades now that you're with Rogers and Cowan."

"Ugh," Robin muttered. Adrian was standing behind him now, massaging Robin's temples. "I thought that's what I had them for."

"Yeah, you need to be discreet."

"What's Rogers and Cowan?" Jesse asked, naively.

"A public relations firm," Robin explained. "They unrolled Caitlyn Jenner. Got her on the cover of *Vanity Fair*. They handled Marilyn Monroe once upon a time. Rock Hudson and all that. Attempted damage control for Mel Gibson. Couldn't say that really worked. He's terrible."

"Robin was just cast on a Hulu-only show that nobody watches."

"It's true," Robin said.

"Oh, what's it called?"

"*South Slope*," he said.

"Horrible," Adrian added, "it's a horrible show," at which Robin nodded, seriously, in agreement.

When Adrian and Robin left Jesse alone for the night, he sank down into the swirling heat of the tub, digging his heels into the cement base as his shoulders pressed into the corner of the in-ground cutout. He massaged his back by rolling back and forth for a few seconds, sipping experimentally from his second drink.

He lay his head back and looked up towards the faint flickerings in the night sky. He wanted so badly for there to be a world out there, unseen to him, but with a real stake in the natural order, sympathetic towards his tortured will. He had free choice to get blind drunk, drown himself, set his car on fire, hurt other people or help them. An old paranoia came to mind, one that only appeared in his darkest moments: that the trivial details of his life, kind actions, patience, the value of human life and compassion itself, none of it meant anything without something beyond to mark its value, just as paper currency would only hold value against the security of a gold standard.

He walked a loop of the exterior of the pool, eyeing an untouched fifth of vodka that lay in a half-melted ice bucket. The bar bill had been paid. The folded leatherette receipt lay beside. There was more than enough vodka in the bottle to bring him towards oblivion. He carried it back to his room so he could drink how he wanted.

He stood on his balcony, dissociating, for almost an hour. He sat down facing the railing, legs crossed, swigging again from the bottle. He was undeniably drunk.

His lips felt cold, the vodka froze his tongue. It was so creamy and numbing. He laughed to himself, then laughed at that. He squinted then rose up, teetering. His foot bashed the divider inside the door. "Fucking. Not. Good!" he yelled. He let his weight take him into a bounce on the mattress. He still had the vodka bottle and reached for the remote, finding a music-only hip-hop station. He sipped and nodded along.

A song he liked came on and he put his hands in the air, waving the bottle around, singing the few words he knew. His foot pulsed with pain, and he got the idea to take painkillers now to burn off the ache tomorrow. When he unzipped his bathroom case he saw the prescription of opioids he'd received through the hospital. He immediately popped one, then brushed his teeth, gargled mouthwash. He could feel himself thinking, but couldn't be certain of any of its meaning.

He slopped into flip-flops and staggered across the courtyard, drunker than he realized. He felt hungry and horny and irritated, restless for something. He claimed his seat upon a high barstool, taking all of his focus to hold it together, acting like he wasn't already drunk. His plans for the future extended hardly beyond one motor movement to the next. Two girls were seated to his right, ignoring cans of beer, staring into their phones, while another couple picked over their vegetable bowls, drinking seltzer.

"Beer," Jesse said, to a bartender who seemed about his age.

He turned to the girl beside him, an alluring blur of a tan line and brown hair. She had a thin necklace that lay across her collarbones.

"Do ya want a beer?"

"What?"

"Do you want a beer? Another beer." He heard himself struggling to put the words in order. A final thrust of reason suggested he turn around and get himself back to his room, put to bed.

"No, I'm good, actually," she said. He turned away, staring blankly ahead. "Hey, sorry," she said again. He turned again and looked at her with what he felt to be a kind, interested look. "You have, like, something on your face?" she said. "Toothpaste or something?"

He resented her so much for saying so. He squinted at his blurred reflection in the bar mirror then wiped his mouth furiously with his arm.

"Yeah, I think you got it."

He looked at her again, thinking she wasn't very cute for her curtness. He thought of Mars, and the sobering realization that if she'd appeared at this moment he'd have no excuse for being so drunk. Paranoia rushed that she might in fact be here. He turned and scanned the sun-cooked crowd, the open-air design of the bar. Guests were shoving each other into the pool, sending splashes and screams into the cool desert air, and he felt the whole night was there with its possibilities. He felt a hot rush through his core, wishing he could become sober and start to get drunk all over again.

One of the girls went to the bathroom, leaving an empty stool next to him. The friendlier one leaned over. "Where are you visiting from?" she asked loudly, over the music, though it was far from what he heard.

"Yeah that was me, I got shot," he said, responding to an imaginary question. He palmed his wound as if it had started to ache. In his other hand he made a pistol shape, and turned it sideways and pointed it at the bartender. "Doot. Doot. Doot. DOOT!" He was wasted.

"Oh, yeah I could," she said. "Two?" She put her fingers up to the bartender, who was pouring shots.

"Don't point that thing at me," the bartender said coolly.

"Wow, rude," her friend said, feeling left out, scooting her stool back out and butting back in. Jesse sensed he needed to reign in his behavior if he was going to get anywhere making friends.

The bartender set out four shot glasses and filled them with tequila, garnishing each with a slice of orange. He put out a shaker of ground cinnamon, and Jesse watched the girls lick a spot on their hands then pour a small amount of the spice. They licked at it, downed the shot, then bit the orange.

"Hey, friend, keep up!" They stared at him, and he knew he would have to keep it cool. He lifted the shot glass and took a brief sip to prepare, though he felt his throat quake and his mouth water, and immediately got a sense he would vomit. He set the shot back down, though it spilled, the liquid running onto the black stone bar.

"If you can't hold it up, you can't drink it," the bartender said, winking at the girls. He sopped up the mess. Jesse was too drunk to feel embarrassed, but kept quiet. He stared into the blur of backlit bottles.

"Sorry," he said, "been at it for a long time today." He watched as the bartender filled a pint of water from the faucet and set it down in front of him. Then he felt a hand reaching into his pocket. One of the girls was rustling. He fumbled in after her and felt a small plastic bag.

"Be quick," she said.

He stared at his reflection in the mirror, then looked around at the expensive soap, the hand towels, the flickering scented candle that smelled like a fireplace. He snapped the little bag a few times with his finger and thumb, then dumped a small clump onto the meat of his balled-up hand, a ritual not dissimilar to the shots the girls had just done. He did one huge inhale, then repeated the process. He ran water on his face and hair, though before he left, he decided to go for a third, even bigger bump than the first two. He felt able to complete a thought by the time he was through.

"Good," he said when he was back. "That's good stuff." He was disappointed they seemed to be leaving right as he started to feel like himself again. One of the girls handed him his beer as they led him out.

"Let's go back to our spot and chill," she said.

The girls explained they'd been in town for a bachelorette party. Jesse wondered what they wanted from him. Intoxication led him down a path toward ego gratification, centered on asking "what can I get?" and determined to find out. He walked with a limp; he had probably broken a toe or two. A bruise was forming on top of his foot. He caught one of the girls eyeing him with suspicion.

They had rented a room with a large outdoor patio, centered around a fire pit and large cushioned seating. One of the girls was playing music off her phone, fixing drinks from the mini fridge. The other cut up lines for them on one of the hotel info guide sleevelets. Jesse was laying back, looking at a blur of stars, but perked up when he saw the chance to do more coke. One of the girls was trying on outfits, popping in and out, while the other cuddled up next to him. He came to understand they might kiss soon, and they did. He became distracted and wondered what she may have been thinking, what she wanted from him, though she soon got up and went into the room, to talk to her friend. "Are we really gonna have a threesome with this guy?" he heard her say.

He was too fucked up to feel nervous and on too many drugs to actually go through with it. The other girl came out and sat down, asking how he was feeling. She had a tank top on over her bathing suit. He thought she looked impossibly cute. He began kissing her, and felt her hand on his thigh. He feared it wasn't of much use; he'd gone numb from the waist down.

"Did you spill water—" she said. He looked down. It must have been the quantity of liquor and drugs, and wasn't there a pill he took hours ago? He couldn't be sure, but he'd just pissed himself. She jolted up, repulsed, taking a step away from him.

"Oh...shit," he said. He stood up and turned away from her, and since he was facing the side door out he just left and stumbled back to his room in deep shame.

Jesse missed his alarm. The curtains were rolled down, and air conditioner blasted against the rising late-morning heat. He awoke at eleven a.m. to a call from an unfamiliar number—it was Judd—telling Jesse he wanted to meet at The Parker for lunch in an hour. There were six missed calls from Mars. Several empty airplane bottles were scattered on the nightstand and he remembered the drinks he'd had before bed. An acidic smell wafted and he rolled over to vomit next to the bed. He hobbled and made it to the bathroom for a few more heaves. Pain radiated through his foot, up his leg. His head felt concussed.

"Fuck," he said, spitting. "This is bad." His foot was brightly bruised up and swollen; he was limping. His phone rang again and it was Mars.

"What's up?!" she asked, sounding offensively revived. "I'm just here with Savannah...from *The Times*?" *Fuck*, he thought, *fuck, fuck, fuck.*

"Yeah," he said, acting his best method-act of a well-rested version of himself. "Just need coffee and stuff. Brushing my teeth now."

"Oh—kay?" she said, straining not to let anything on, as if Savannah might read into it. Then he remembered the bar, the girls, and deep shame settled. He was still in his clothes. He'd have to shower. To bolt the door and set a roaring fire in his room seemed the simplest way to solve his problems. What if he just went back to bed? He brushed his teeth under the shower head, knowing it was the best he would feel all day, in that womblike massage of streams.

He'd only packed dress clothes and beach wear. His brown dress shoes were the only footwear he could put on to disguise his injury, though that required long pants, and he only had his suit. He still felt drunk, hobbling into the shoes, buttoning up the dirty shirt. A look in the mirror back at his red, hungover eyes brought up a squelch of tears. He felt alone and lost at sea. He choked down the lump in his throat and reached for his sunglasses. He'd staved off hangovers in his earlier teens, in fact they'd hardly registered, and this was something new. He felt an unwelcome rush of anxiety and emotion. He looked through his phone, trying to patch the night together. He hadn't texted Mars, but had an incoming call from his dad, which made no sense, then he remembered his own call. Was he already drunk then? A layer of sweat coated his skin. Something to deal with later.

The outfit did help him play the part a bit, and when he saw Mars was in a floral sundress, he didn't feel his choice was too absurd. He masked his limp, kept his distance upon greeting Savannah. So far, so good. Mars had called for a car, Savannah seemed eager to start getting material from Jesse. He needed to say something.

"Sorry if I seem out of it, I don't see color until I've had coffee." Jesse hid behind his sunglasses, probably quoting his uncle. "The world is simply black and white through a Vaseline lens."

Mars shot him a concerned look; he realized he was trying too hard. Then one of the desk managers caught Jesse's attention.

"Sir," she said, putting pressure on the word, waving him over while the others weren't looking. "So you're...sticking around today?" Jesse had never seen this woman before. "Maybe you don't remember," she said, looking past him, and Jesse felt a new wave of anxiety wash over him. "You walked out on your tab. It was two whiskeys." Jesse tried to make sense of it; he remembered being at the bar, but this didn't track. "You were piss drunk."

"I remember being out a bit in the evening," Jesse mumbled.

"Guy with a broken toe?"

"Okay, yeah." The valet was waving down their ride to lunch. Mars was flagging Jesse to come get in.

"The shift manager called me into the bar because you stumbled in blackout drunk around midnight." Her tone had taken on an edge. "You tried to steal a wine bottle from the bar. You couldn't even walk. It took two of us to get you to your room."

"Jesus," Jesse said. He was actually horrified.

"Yeah, you were sobbing, disturbing some of the other residents. You begged me to call you an Uber back to LA. You demanded to check out and leave. Then, you cursed me out when I couldn't do it." The façade of customer service had been removed—she was pissed.

"Alright, what do I need to do?" He could be in a holding cell right now, waiting to blow 0.00.

"I need you out of here as soon as possible."

"Jesssseeeeee!" Mars sang out the window.

"As soon as possible. I will. Okay." He didn't dare look her in the eyes, and instead made for the car, where none of this had ever happened.

Mars looked over at him sweetly and sadly.

"Bitsy died." Mars showed Jesse a picture from Rosie Pig's feed. It was from a funeral, and showed Rosie Pig up on her back legs, leaning on a casket. It was macabre, hilarious actually, and Mars choked her chuckles as Jesse processed what had happened.

"What. The. Fuck," he mouthed. "How?"

"No idea," Mars said. "Probably OD'd. I can try to get in touch with her sister." She wasn't joking. Savannah and Jesse were sitting on either side of Mars, though when Mars saw her making a note, she tucked her phone out of sight. Jesse rolled the window down and let the desert air cool his nausea.

Judd was waiting for them in the lobby, and he expressed annoyance when he realized Savannah was trailing them for a story, though once they were seated quickly enough at the outdoor patio—away from the other guests—the issue was closed.

There was no icebreaker. Jesse blabbered nervously, on autopilot, poorly introducing himself, poorly explaining he was hoping to break in as a screenwriter. He prayed he wouldn't throw up right on the table. Savannah took notes as her iPhone recorded their conversation. Judd kept his aviators on as he ordered a chopped cobb salad; Mars ordered a Bellini, skipping food, and Jesse ordered fajitas. Mars cast him a quick, disapproving look over the simplicity of his choice. Savannah ordered a cup of coffee. Judd listened patiently before saying his piece.

"So, eighty-four percent of shows fail, is that what you wanted to hear? Or a phrase like 'quality scripts on time?' Or that showrunning is choreography? Why don't you take a night class, or one of those three-day seminars?" Jesse felt humiliated. Savannah had temporarily stopped writing.

Mars was looking at her phone, swatting an invisible fly.

"I'm working on the show scripts now, it's called *Count the Waves*," Jesse said, moving to the only half-planned part of his speech. He gave a refined version of the pitch he'd given Ryan Seacrest a month ago from the hospital bed. Judd sunk into his chair, nodded as Jesse spoke, then finally responded.

"If you just get it in front of people, it would probably do well, but there's a lifetime of obstacles between now and then," he said, "and I don't know if I can help you. Why do you want to be a writer, anyway? Be an actor. Don't you want to watch your girlfriend take a shower outside on a yacht?"

"Sure," Jesse said, wishing that Judd would simply pretend to want to help him as a favor.

Savannah saved him by asking Mars about her writing career, which Jesse knew so little about.

"Yeah, I wrote a book of poems when I was nineteen. That's it," she said, then switched the topic. "I love TV, sure, I've thought of ideas. I have this whole idea for a Texas noir set in the Hill Country, where I grew up. One of the main characters is a drone hobbyist, and he catches this murder in HD on his drone camera. Small town chaos ensues, you know, the usual. It's so green and lush there, really pretty, and everyone's so fucked up, there's so much emotion and drama among the dried up bluebonnets and vineyards and, I don't know, broken down lives. Everyone's got their hustle. Sex workers and palm readings and dirty cops and all that."

Judd seemed taken by Mars and her idea, which was admittedly better than Jesse's, who felt crushed by his inability to convey them: he'd face-planted. Savannah scribbled notes. Mars asked Judd about his film *Funny People*, challenging him on the idea that rich people suffer their problems more acutely because they have the rest of life's exigencies figured out.

"Yes," Judd said, in response, "well, I believe there is truth to that. And I know people want to say, 'Oh, they have a nice house, they have wealth, they can't suffer,' but it's simply not true."

She'd put him on the defensive, and worse, Jesse saw her getting a bit upset.

"Well," she said, running her finger around the base of the chalice—for her second drink she'd ordered a Rose Kennedy: gin and seltzer with a splash of cranberry. "People with money have more solutions available for their problems. More options, a huge net to fall into. Who cares about unhappy successful people whose misery is set only against their career goals?"

"Ah," Judd said, almost flirting with her, or daring her to go on. "So the poet-turned-actress has a platform." He seemed done with the conversation, and began opening emails on his phone.

"An ethics has to sting. Otherwise you're just another person taking up bulk. I was at a birthday party for a friend at the Chateau Marmont recently. You know how you can order DVDs and CDs from the lobby? So people are crashing and it's like four a.m. and they 'ring up the porter' to bring us *Blue Jasmine*. Problem is I've sworn off Woody Allen, and I can't watch it. But I want to. I love Cate Blanchett and everyone's buzzing about this film. Anyways, I leave, making up some excuse, and that stung. It stung making up an excuse, to my friend, who is sober, who wanted to have a slumber party for her girlfriends, who were smashed off the drinks tray. I wasn't trying to make a queen scene out of it. But that's honest living."

"I think empathy is important," Judd said to Savannah, trying to behave after realizing he could end up in a jam if he left an unfavorable impression. "*Funny People* could be seen as a treatise on that."

"I disagree," Mars said. "I think that is an immature, 'golden rule' idea of society. Isn't it more empathetic, more truthful, that it may be our differences—not our similarities—that make up the roots of our existence?"

"So if a member of the one percent writes beautiful poetry, it has no value to you?"

"Rich people should not write poetry," Mars said, probably just to say it, at which Jesse laughed and Savannah seemed to as well, covering her mouth after taking a sip of coffee. "Jesse, do you want to tell Savannah about your script for the game?" Mars asked, with genuine enthusiasm.

"No, actually," he said, sadly. "I'm not so sure about any of that at the moment." He continued, "I've actually spent the day resisting the idea that my enthusiasm was not going to be enough to make it in screenwriting." He looked around the grounds from his seat and tried to take in the fresh air, compartmentalizing his anxiety, as he'd learned on a meditation podcast, prioritizing the sweet and sour perfume from the gardens of lush flowers and hidden pools. A mother was holding up a chubby toddler high in the air, speaking in a baby voice, then turned it around, smelling its ass through the heavy diaper.

"My son played this game recently," Savannah then said, speaking for the first time. "I can't remember the name, but it's one of those apocalypse games, and it had this great story, I mean really great. I sat there with my daughter watching him play it, thinking the whole time, so many of these kids are exposed to these narratives. In this game there's a black kid and white kid helping each other fight to live, you see them suffer, experience pain. You see as they see and are seen. I think that can go a long way, especially in that formative age range."

"Jesse's game is like that," Mars said. "It takes mental conditions, mental illnesses, and projects them onto your environment, in this totally cool, dramatic way, using all of the horror movie tropes, and you have to keep yourself alive. And the actual point is to empathize with the character you choose, with their issues, so you can keep them alive. And so you start to understand different types of people, all as a byproduct of playing this rad game." She seemed truly proud that Jesse had thought it through as much as he had. Savannah even smiled as she made a note. But Jesse wasn't present for it. All he could think of was the NDA he'd signed, how he shouldn't have told Mars anything. In the perfect silence of the midday calm he abruptly excused himself to the bathroom to go dry heave.

The physical space brought relief. If only he could spend the day floating on a raft in The Chateau's pool, away from the world. For now he settled for splashing water on his face. He laughed into the mirror, patted hand towels over his cheeks to dry off. For all his immediate struggles, he felt he looked handsome. He took a few deep breaths as a stranger began to talk to him.

"Do you want a Xanax bar or something?" It was David Schwimmer, looking over at him with concern in his eyes.

"Uh, yeah sure," Jesse said. Instead of handing it to him, he dropped it into the side pocket of Jesse's blazer, as if there were anything illicit about the deal.

"Do you think having family in the industry could help him?" Savannah asked Judd, as Jesse finished up in the bathroom.

"Who's the family?" Judd asked.

"His mother was Patricia Shore," she said, flipping through her notes. "She passed almost a decade ago."

Judd turned this over as it clicked in his mind. "Bernie's kid? That's Jesse Shore? Sure, I know Bernie. He's writing that great network show that's on now. *Greetings*. You know, about the flight attendants working out of O'Hare. Sort of a contemporary *Pan Am* or *Wings*. It's great. What the shit does he need me for?"

Savannah was writing and grinning.

"I don't think he knows that," Mars said. "They're sort of estranged."

Judd got up impatiently to leave as he spotted Jesse coming back from the bathroom.

"Look," Judd said to him, squinting through his sunglasses, laptop bag slung over his shoulder. "If you want to break in, write an episode of a show you really love, like really love, and truly know. Sit at home in a comfy chair and do some writing for free in your pajamas. Write an episode of...*Retinue*, or something."

"Poolside," Jesse said, snapping unexpectedly.

"Why not." Judd shrugged, dismissively. "And if you need an idea for your photoshoot, here's a free one." He turned back to them, his laptop bag slung over his shoulder. "I had dinner with my daughter at Soho House the other night. She was going to meet friends later, dressed up in all this designer hoo-haw, Balmain, Saint Laurent. It looked like armor. You know, tactical armor?"

"That is almost cynical enough to work for the paper-of-note," Savannah said, after he'd gone.

"Yeah, I mean," Mars said, "is that what you need?"

"Unfortunately, yes," Savannah said. "It's, um, well my editor always redirects these pieces into a sort of, slant-looking, backhanded article." Jesse's alarm went off. It was noon and he needed to post a photo online. The property had plenty of photo-ready vistas, though he was in no shape to hike the grounds in search of them. A food picture was out of the question as he'd been pushing his food around to try and make it look half-eaten, resulting in meaty slop. The only thing of interest around him was Mars, who protested when he lifted his phone camera to snap her photo, though fearing Savannah, she lowered her guard, batted her lashes, making a playful spectacle of it, before switching to a three-quarter glance, her smile only a hint. *Maybe she's born with it, maybe she's Marsy-Rose Arenas*, he wrote, before uploading.

Mars, A.D.

By <u>Savannah Williams</u>

"An ethics has to sting," Mars told a famous television producer, who strained his ears over a boozy lunch at The Parker in Palm Springs. I trailed the actress on a pitch session, which was playing out in the foreground of the property's famous gardens. Mars, née Marsy-Rose Arenas, played more of a supporting role to her new friend, Jesse Shore, an aspiring screenwriter whose meet-cute was occasioned by the force-majeure: he survived the same shooting Mars did, and they began corresponding shortly after.

Mars recently blasted into the spotlight after news reported she was struck in the shoulder while trying to have a book signed by Kim Kardashian West (think of a less successful Christina Grimmie situation) as a birthday present for her 11-year-old brother, who she says has a crush on Kim. Yesterday she gave a speech supporting gun control, sharing a bill with her off-again fling Marc Pevier.

While she hasn't been on the cover of *Vogue*, yet, she's just wrapped a shoot with Balmain, shot by Camilla Akrans (whose image of Rihanna recently blessed the cover of *Bazaar*). Next week Mars is reuniting with old friend Mario Testino, who shot her first major campaign nearly 10 years ago for French fashion house Givenchy. With her wide forehead and low-set, thick, feral eyebrows, bright green eyes, perfect pout, hard jaw, slender, slight frame, and poreless complexion, Mars could easily be placed in the top one percent of the world's most beautiful people, by worldwide standards.

"It's totally obvious cynicism is the dominant mode of our time," she said to me, riding back to Los Angeles from the desert. She'd flown in from New York and opted not to rent a car. "I have a license, but I hate driving," she explained, her attention diving and surfacing in and out of her iPhone, which was encased in a large, pale pink rubber case shaped like a seashell. "I have to have a drink or two to feel comfortable behind the wheel."

She alternated between taking videos of the landscape and texting with her 13-year-old sister; they're making plans for their brother's birthday party tomorrow, sans *Selfish*. "I'll have to give him a belated gift this year," she said. She admitted she sends half of the money she earns back home to her family.

The oldest of seven, her dad is in between jobs and her mom teaches kindergarten near their home in Lincoln Heights.

The 31-year-old recently dated Marc Pevier, whose show *Retinue* continues to earn him $200,000 an episode. Mars was reticent on her relationship with Marc, but said the show, while not being able to deny its success and appeal, "reversed feminism" and that "anyone with a B.A. in liberal arts could write about its deteriorating effects, an article-a-day on it."

Jesse, who is writing an episode of the show on spec, lay stretched out behind us in the backseat, a position more fit for a sleeping child, with his phone fallen to the side as he listened to a guided meditation track. I suspect he took some of the THC candy he's prescribed for PTSD. When I suggested the show was a "male version" of *Sex in the City*, Mars responded dryly, saying "the male version of anything is never a good idea."

While Kardashian West's book is mostly entirely made of selfies, Marsy-Rose is quite literate. Considered a poetic phenom as a teen, she published a book titled *Lullaby* at age 19, poems of love and awe occasionally piercing her resolved jadedness with the world at large, punctuated by a long elegy for her high school sweetheart who died in a car accident her senior year. "We'd probably be married if he was still alive," she said. A longtime resident of Los Angeles, she now lives in the Big Apple, coming home regularly enough to see family and, in her words, "let go of the stories the mind makes in New York."

Testino plans to include Jesse in his shoot for Saint Laurent Paris's pre-spring campaign, a collection they developed in response to a string of mass shootings here in the U.S., a concept he said he developed when Hedi Slimane was creative director of the company. The new line riffs on leather pieces from the permanent collection, crossing them with medieval designs for armor that Slimane acquired while visiting Eastern Europe.

"See, that's cynicism," Arenas said, who seemed unconvinced of the gesture, and clarified by saying, "It's cynical of them for thinking that high fashion can do social justice work, when really you're just making cool looking clothes that photograph well. Yet here I am, glamorizing it by letting them use me in the ad." More cynical yet, while her modeling career may be seeing an uptick in opportunities, her age contends with classic Hollywood discrimination and preference for fresh faces. When cast in the footlights as a struggling actress, her milieu seems much less favorable.

Her demo reel shows a similarly strained attempt at making a career of acting, and most noteworthy clips include small parts on popular shows such as *Mad Men* and *30 Rock*, movies such as *Hostel* and *Ballers*. An IMDb search shows over a dozen filmography credits, as well as an appearance on user-generated list "Dazzlingly Beautiful Unknown Actresses II" (adult film title, anyone?).

We're passing the outlets near Covina when Jesse chimes in, "She knows what to say 'yes' to. And, more importantly, when to say 'no.'" Jesse, a television and cinema fanatic, explained he's writing a semi-biographical treatment for a family drama called *Count the Waves* that mirrors the traumas in his own life, starting with the loss of his mother when he was a young teen. Jesse's inspiration is his mother, the late Patricia Shore, who created the Emmy Award-winning miniseries *Until I See Palm Trees Again*, which told the story of her terminal illness and family's preparations for her death. Jesse's father, Bernard Shore, is the creator of *Greetings*, a show currently airing in CBS's show-killing Sunday, 10 p.m. time slot.

Jesse shrugged when I asked him if it was cynical to exploit his autobiography for his art. "It's material I know well," he said. "And it feels good." The only better therapy than writing, Jesse said, is falling asleep in a raft in his uncle's pool as the neighbors bicker about who will grow taller sunflowers that summer.

"I'm far from her biggest fanboy, but I guess I'm seduced by what she represents: beauty, branding, world-class business acumen," Jesse answered when I asked him why he'd gone to meet Kim Kardashian West on that fateful day. "Mostly I just wanted the book as a decoration for my apartment."

"Maybe you can write an episode around the shooting," Mars suggested, looking at him in the rearview mirror. "Maybe," he said skeptically, his mind turning it over. "The thing about TV is you can tell a lot of stories in a show, people are willing to wait to see what's going on with all those plotlines, even though it takes awhile to get to all of them." He looked at the ceiling of the car as we began hitting traffic back into the city. "No, our story would make a better movie."

*A previous version of this story misnamed the show as "Unless I See Palm Trees Again."

Chapter 6: Greetings

You smelled like liquor this morning.

Hmm was probably the vile hotel body wash.

No. But are you okay? What happened?

I made some mistakes I guess. Can we not talk about it?
Really blew that meeting.

Ya you did.
Don't say anything in front of Savannah but
I have to show you something

Ok...?

www.nbc.com/shows/greetings
i think this is your dad's show

Oh...
oh shit

Yeah...Judd told us when you were in the bathroom
did you know about this at all?

Um, no

Don't say anything aloud right now

I won't don't worry

Oh my god
total shock

Sorry, hunno
:-/

Jesse was lying across the backseat of Savannah's car as she drove them home. He was feeling nauseous—his hangover had gotten much worse—and he was hiding his melancholia behind his sunglasses, pretending to nap, the rivers and tides of the body high sending gentle ripples of sensation through his nervous system. On account of some very strong medical-grade edibles he'd just taken, he curled up in the back seat like a child and dwelled involuntarily on memories with his parents.

In the first memory, his mother had taken him to work to the writers' room, where staff encircled a table covered by snacks and drinks. They all looked charmed to have him playing on the floor around them. He was five or six. In the next, his mother was ill; he was visiting her in the hospital. He was seven or eight, oblivious to the seriousness of her condition, and while his father spoke with a doctor in private, Jesse's mother pointed to a snack that was left by a nurse: a container of Utz Potato Stix, which he devoured quickly, licking his fingers. The newest memory was of him riding in the car with his father to his mother's funeral, the radio's obstinate nihilism nattering as his dad held a blank stare a thousand yards through the windshield.

Breathing through the emotional pain of these thoughts, he landed back on the total failure of the meeting he'd just had. He should have used his down time last night making notes and practicing his talking points before getting a good night's sleep and eating a healthy breakfast.

Many of Jesse's fantasias indulged the opposite to these ragged edges of the disappointing narrative life forms—ones that certainly make uninteresting television. That life is necessarily tragic, ending with nothing but a banal or even humiliating string of leftovers, what Virgil referred to as "tears in things," sorry remainders bereft of finality.

By his own choice he'd remained stripped of communication from his father until the call last night. New York City was a playground, a limitless distraction— the constant rendezvous with friends, lazy rocking subway rides and rush hour commutes deferred his attention from the issue. Back home, reminders of his core negative beliefs were everywhere: unkempt and sadly dropping palm fronds, exit signs he'd read countless times. Now he realized the abuse inherent to the slight he'd done to his father. Holding on to this anger at him—for what, remarrying?—was becoming a particularly thin reaction to feeling justified anger after his mother's death. Whatever.

He knew there was a world out there unwanted and abhorred by some, of common use to most, essential to a few. Billboards and magazines, a repertoire of moving images, of cinematic moments, of lives quietly overlaid with projections and entangling fantasias and dramatic storylines. Jesse, that he may live, demanded an active claim in this arena of contradictions. That there was recognition, finally, of life's banalities against less compelling claims and reconstructions towards its value sent Jesse into the welcoming hold of the culture industry, its valorization of capital, mania for money, whirlpool of opaque strategies of persona-making. How celebrities are considered to have actual existence, how he knew more about their families than his own. For all its inducement of bad feelings and shame and usurious emotional manipulations, he was a consumer. And it was necessary to live. He felt a longing for the night. He could hide under cover of whichever vice was necessary, the pool, television on repeat, porn, maybe sneaking a drink or two would make him feel better. Lee wouldn't need to know about last night.

He jolted awake to the soundtrack blasting through Savannah's car speakers. Mars had taken over the stereo and was playing a Sia song, an unfamiliar song that opened like a B-movie flesh wound as they charged through the desert, volume up over the engine of her leased Lexus RX 350 "Pebble Beach Edition." Jesse slid down in the leather backseat—the interior trim specially bleached like white sand— holding his fingers laced behind his head, squinting as his awareness of particulars came into focus through the window; the occasional slow-turning windmill and far-off ridge line, the drought-stunted desert between. It was a barren world. They passed a sign for the outlets.

"Yeah, Jesse loves mediocre films, Paul Schrader's *The Canyons* is probably the starting point. Then *The Bling Ring* and *Somewhere, Lost River*, and um, oh right, *Neon Demon*! This is the song that plays over the credits. I guess it's pretty mediocre too, but when I heard it when the credits started rolling, it gave me chills. I realized I'd watched a ninety-minute fashion editorial. I practically expected the cast to walk out from behind the screen like they were coming on to the catwalk."

"They're orphaned," Jesse said, over the music. "They're not good enough to want to have a second viewing, no one really wants to talk about them. They aren't bad enough to become kitsch objects. They're just left behind."

Savannah asked Mars about her writing, would she consider returning to it, if even a memoir about her twenties in the industry, maybe something light. Mars grimaced.

"No, literally never. Those days are over. I haven't written in ten years." He noticed ire in her tone.

Jesse had never written a poem in his life, and he couldn't be sure if he'd ever read one. He began texting Mars, who he could see in the side view mirror.

Poem for Mars:

I'd rather be with you
sitting at a table
waiting for tonight

He'd lost his car, becoming an Angeline castrato. His phone died while he was getting drunk last night and he was charging it off Savannah's console. He received an admonishing email from his boss, whom he'd never met. The bag of unread novels lay mockingly on the floor mat beside him, overdue a week now, and he hadn't even started the first of them. He wrote back lying about internet woes on top of traveling, then accessed the shared spreadsheet using his phone and wrote a series of "maybe" and "no," indiscriminately. He had missed calls and had a voicemail from Lee that he was too fearful to listen to. He deleted it without listening, then sent Lee a text: *On my way back now.*

It may come to that, Mars texted Jesse back. *My family is on the west side for the day and there might not be anyone sober enough to drive them back by the time rush hour is over.*

Jesse looked back at his words, an altar to his feelings, or shrine to their circumstances.

Mars texted back, *What actually are you up to tonight? I'm feeling more social than I was last night.*

"What do you have planned for your...your brother's birthday, tomorrow, is it?" Savannah asked, butting into what she believed was still Mars' text conversation with her sister.

"Uh, BBQ in Lincoln Park with the family," she said vacantly. "Shit. I never figured out his gift. Fuck."

Tonight just hanging at The Chateau, Jesse texted back.

"Are you in touch with your family a lot?" Savannah asked Mars.

"Constantly," Mars responded. "My sister needs me. My mom is sort of against anything that makes life easier for teenage girls."

"Such as?"

"I'm talking to her about birth control now."

Mars' phone rang; it was Mable, the sister she'd been texting with for most of the ride. She answered on speaker.

"Hello—I'm sort of busy," she said in that matter-of-fact way that one necessarily takes with family.

"Zack doesn't know who Emily Ratajkowski is!" yelled Mable with the frenetic power unique to teenagers.

"So?"

"Tell him how famous she is!"

"Well she was in that video," Savannah stated encouragingly, trying to help. "What was that song called?"

"That's what I said!" Mable shot back over the phone. Her voice sounded frolicking and unbound. "He says he's never even heard that song."

"She was in that movie with what's his name," Savannah said again. "Not Matt Damon, the other one."

"*Gone Girl*," Jesse said from the back.

"Was that her? That sidepiece?" Mars said.

"Yeah, she's everywhere!" Mable said. "Are you coming over tomorrow for the party?"

"I thought that was tonight?"

"Got to go," she yelled again, then giggled at something unrelated to the call and hung up.

At The Chateau, Jesse knew something unusual was going on by way of the errant arrangement of vehicles. The seashell metallic Volvo wagon was parked closest to the garage door with an unfamiliar rental behind it. A roadster was on the street in the spot where he would have normally parked the Miata. He suddenly wondered if it was Lee's birthday.

A van with decals from Pale Pink Farm—an intimate, fifty-seat American heritage fare restaurant with its own garden—idled temporarily at a jutted half-parked angle in the driveway. A man holding a large delivery was waiting for someone to open the door. Most macabre was Bitsy's car, which remained parked across the street on the side of a neighboring property. Jesse thought how bleak it was to see she'd stuck lavish vinyl letters spelling out Rosie Pig's website across on her back window.

As Jesse helped Mars with her bags, the anxiety that accompanied his anticipation flipped to dread when he saw his stepmother Cheryl moving things around in the kitchen. It could only mean his father was there too, and Jesse's heart nearly went out when it was he who opened the door to receive the food.

Jesse unloaded their luggage, then checked his phone to see if he'd somehow missed a call from Uncle Lee. He realized the texts he'd sent hours ago hadn't gone through; they must have been passing through a dead spot when he texted him to say he'd be arriving with a guest. His father was heavier, grayer, wearing a yellow polo shirt and khaki shorts, the uniform he'd lived his life in. He'd put on some "happy weight" in the year or so since they'd seen one another. He'd grown a handsome beard, had a better haircut, which Jesse read as indicators of his successful move back in the television industry.

Cheryl had dyed her hair a soft lavender and wore it in short, feathered layers with a wispy fringe. She appeared behind Bernie to help bring the large plastic bags containing the boxed catering, but froze when she saw Jesse, who struggled to haul his tote of books over his shoulder while he balanced his shabby nylon pack cloth weekender bag on Mars' wheeled aluminum carry-on. Mars politely mimed goodbye as Savannah zipped off to a dinner in Koreatown, anxious to beat traffic as night rose out of the puce sunset.

Food and luggage delayed the opportunity for Jesse to either hug his father or perpetuate their long-standing silence a moment or two longer, and he peevishly turned to Mars, who was trotting to catch up as they crossed the threshold of The Chateau together. He awkwardly marshaled her downstairs to his room in the back of the house, though on his way he found his sober mentor and The Chateau's next-door neighbor Daffy, in a bright Hawaiian shirt, then Lee, standing beside him, near the open back door to the pool.

"Hello, Jesse," Daffy said.

"What's going on here?" he said.

"Well, some bad news," Lee said.

"Lee was having some chest pains so we went to the ER last night."

"Something of a mild heart attack," Lee said, looking past Daffy to Jesse. The plaintive expression in his eyes told a more serious truth. His eyes were wet and Jesse suddenly felt very uncomfortable. Lee's demeanor was shifting in his presence, and Daffy rubbed Lee's back with wide open-handed strokes.

"I feel like I've been walking through Jell-O, pain in my chest, dizziness—"

"I'll fill him in—" Daffy cut him off. Jesse felt very much like a child watching adults deliberate. Then there was the issue of his dad.

Lee went inside, though turned, and frowned, bracing against the threshold. "Have you spoken to your father?" he asked.

Jesse lifted his hands in defense, backing up a step. "I planned to call him tonight, as soon as I was free, I swear—"

Lee cut him off, rolling his eyes. It was one of the few times Jesse had seen him show stone-cold impatience.

"It's heart disease," Daffy said. "For all of his health, they could only say it was"— a heavy pause—"genetic." Jesse still couldn't speak, and he realized how bad he was with tragic news, his mind always rushing to need to tell someone.

Daffy turned to Mars, then back to Jesse, and said, "I'll make myself useful inside." Jesse felt unable to face Mars; he was crying. She swaddled him in a hug, and he enjoyed the perverse pleasure of it, wishing to stay there forever, rather than endure the next few hours, as he expected they were to reset the course of his life. "You still really smell like liquor."

The large family style portions unboxed old memories and their concomitant bad feelings: Jesse remembered how Lee had belligerently over-ordered from restaurants in the week after his mom passed while the family grieved together. The scene was again set for crisis as large serving bowls filled the dining room table: servings for ten to twelve people each of grilled endive, shaved fennel, vegetable risotto, roasted hatch chili corn pudding, braised chard, harvest succotash, brussels sprouts with pancetta, mussels in saffron broth, thick-cut pork chop, grilled monkfish, poached cherries, butterscotch budino, salt and molasses cookie crumbles, whipped cream—he'd departed from one locus of affluence three hours ago and landed upon another equally sensational one. Abundance constituted the negation of scarcity, a symbol of the attempt to shore up what was left against the inevitable, handing around one compostable set of bamboo cutlery at a time to save the bereaved the trouble of extra cleaning.

"Hey, dad," Jesse said, stepping into the room. He'd showered and brushed his teeth twice, anything to wipe clean the smell of his relapse. He was less afraid of his father than Daffy, and Lee most of all.

"Jesse," he said, his voice cracked to a whisper. They squeezed into a quick but secure hug, and Jesse had no sense of what to say. "The last time I saw you was in a picture, online." His eyebrows raised, convecting consternation over seeing his son in news stories and tabloid articles and gossip sites over the past month, a week's development at a time. "Is the individual you're with the other half of this media dalliance?"

"Marsy-Rose Arenas," Jesse said, letting the syllables fill his mouth.

"She goes by Mars," Cheryl said.

"And she's an actress..." Bernie affirmed while examining a clean plate.

"She's done a lot of things here and there," Jesse liaised on her behalf. "*The Times* is writing this long feature about us, actually," he added, rushing to the disclosure.

"I heard that," Bernie said, sounding apprehensive. "And what's their angle here?"

"Honestly, I think it's going to be mostly about her," Jesse said.

"Sounds like that's for the better, considering," Bernie said. *Considering what*, Jesse pinched a smirk, though could only guess how it had looked to his father: depicted as a cocaine-using party boy, a THC addict and possible adulterer. Jesse couldn't have been more pleased to be branded alongside the a sultry fuck-ups he admired: River Phoenix, Robert Downey Junior. He thought of Mars' comments about cynicism. And he could turn the narrative once things settled down and he recovered, even if it was a lie.

Lee appeared dressed for dinner.

"How are you feeling?" Daffy asked, straight away.

"Rested, better," he said, sitting down. He looked as he always did, trim, with his shirt tucked neatly into his pants.

Mars ascended the stairs to the main floor wearing a Stella McCartney satin bomber jacket over a cream blouse, black Rag and Bone jeans, pink Opening Ceremony creepers. Jesse felt his heart crack; his attraction to Mars was somehow deeply encoded into his unconscious, only understandable on a genetic level, or beyond: if there was a God, the explanation may only lie there.

Cheryl dug around the fridge and found a very cold bottle of wine, which she placed on the table, so close to Jesse. The sound of the cork un-glunking ignited a second coming of his hangover, and he started to think how good a glass would feel right now. He could smell fruit spritzing in the air, and the label equally seduced him with its elegant foil script. He watched Mars tumble wine into her glass, then have a quick sip. He was staring.

"What?" she mouthed. Then she looked back at her glass as if she'd done something unacceptable.

Lee nudged Jesse on the arm then. "Your father doesn't want to tell you this, but it's his wedding anniversary." He said it loud enough that it became a mandatory subject. Jesse feared they would raise a toast, though no one seemed particularly up for it.

The details of his father's second marriage ceremony remained apocryphal. Jesse hadn't attended, of course, and only a few of Cheryl's family were present. He'd remained willfully oblivious to any details of their life.

"Where was it?" Mars asked, reasonably.

"East Hampton," Cheryl said. "It's embarrassing to admit, but I fell in love with the region because of Ina Garten."

"It's gorgeous," Mars said, anticipating a needed solidarity with Cheryl.

"The paths were creamy with meadowsweet and the air heavy with all the scents of summer," Lee recited. "It was a day of peculiar splendor." He trailed off.

Jesse scanned the table, watching Mars twirl her wine glass. She was drinking very slowly. Neither his father nor Cheryl had touched theirs at all.

"Elms, sycamores, horse chestnuts," Bernie added, rubbing Cheryl's hand.

"It's a certain kind of paradise," Mars said, sadly, meditating on the piss-yellow liquid in her glass.

Jesse imagined himself taking ahold of his and downing it in two easy gulps.

"It is," Cheryl sighed. "It's far from Chicago." She separated the meat of a mussel from its shell. "We've buried ourselves in work."

"We have," Bernie agreed.

"I hear you're working on a new show that's on television right now?" Mars asked.

"That's correct," Bernie warmed to her. "Cheryl is a co-creator and writer too, actually."

"Have you seen it?" Cheryl asked Mars, as Jesse swallowed the news of their collaboration.

Mars shook her head no, wiping her mouth with a cloth napkin, then quickly explained, "I haven't gotten to yet. You know, you received a charming endorsement from, what-was-his-name? He told us all about it."

"Judd Apatow," Jesse said.

"Ah. And since when do you know Judd Apatow?" Bernie asked, skeptically.

"Since he fucking rear ended me!" Jesse yelled. Lee shot him a disapproving look.

"*Tranquilo*," Mars purred, rubbing his shoulder as one would stroke the nervousness from an animal. Jesse was beginning to feel like a child among adults.

"I believe there's an automobile accident in one of the recent episodes of *Greetings*," Lee said. "It's the character I've always understood to be based on you, Jesse."

Jesse didn't try to hide his unease while Lee continued. Mars had a big sip of wine, finally, then topped herself back off. It was maddening for him to watch. He made up his mind to sneak some later, if only medicinally to feel better.

"Yes, a character is driving drunk, I believe, at sixteen, and somehow wrecks his car into, what was it, a Neiman Marcus, or something like that, one of those stores anchoring a shopping mall. So, he hits a water pipe and floods the lobby. It's very Aaron Spelling." Lee's hands circled in the air as he spoke.

"Ooh," Mars sang. "A character based on Jesse?" she teased. "What else does this character do?"

"Jesse's louche behavior has made quite a spectacle in several media formats," Lee boomed unexpectedly, joining the conversation more now that he'd regained his composure. "I know he's cost you a bit of money in the past but we needn't make him suffer that now in front of our guest," he added, in a show of compassion.

"No," Bernie said defiantly. "Cheryl paid the entire settlement out of pocket. I'd invested Patricia's life insurance into the business, of course I hadn't written anything in years, in fact in those days I didn't think I would ever work as a writer again. They put me on a medical leave of absence." He spoke with the unaffected distance of someone who'd put such an incident behind them. "Cheryl brought it back to me, or me back to it, whichever way it goes. We all owe her."

"Well, none of that on my watch," Daffy said. Jesse couldn't look anyone in the eye.

"Look, I haven't been drinking," Jesse said. "I think I deserve some credit."

"You haven't been calling me either," Daffy said. "But, good job not drinking."

The lie held intoxicating power. He felt Mars kick him under the table. He jolted, and everyone noticed. He shot her a very dirty look, daring her to outright betray him. No one said anything else on the topic.

Lee turned his attention to Mars, and over dessert they discussed their interview at *The Times*, the accident with Judd, Jesse's inability to hold a job, and the state of his project with Marilyn Manson, who was trying to get a hold of Jesse and had left a message with Lee saying so.

"I'd better call him right back," Jesse said in a tone. He felt very put on the spot and uncomfortable, and was eager to get away from the group as soon as possible.

"There's something else I need to tell everyone," Lee said now. "I'm putting the house on the market, to see what happens. The house is being appraised first thing tomorrow morning so, I didn't want it to be a surprise." He was talking now to Jesse, who felt devastated that the door to the secret garden he'd delighted in almost all of his conscious life would be sealed forever.

❧

Separate spot fires joined overnight with the "Old Fire" in Calabasas, and the arch of the dusty plume widened beneath the blue spell of dusk. A crescent moon embellished the sky. Planes circled Inglewood. On the back patio alone, on the phone with Marilyn, Jesse sat on a chaise, becoming animated at hearing the project had now fallen through entirely.

"You fucking asshole," Jesse shouted, "you've absolutely fucked me," taking out a month's buildup of anger in this moment. Marilyn let him have it out, then countered with another unexpected offer.

"It's either an easy cash grab or golden opportunity for a young man such as yourself," Marilyn had put it, in his droll, talky way.

He'd received a call from an entertainment company that was building out a haunted house on Manhattan's Lower East Side—the team had split with the creative director after conflicts about money—and they were looking for new narrative outlines that fit their structure. Marilyn thought Jesse's script could easily be adopted, and suggested he be brought on as creative director, a position including an apartment in the city with a stipend. He'd have to be in New York through October, beginning immediately. "Doors open the same day pumpkin spice lattes hit menus." He recommended confirming his decision no later than the next morning.

"All that's solid goes into air," Daffy recited from beyond the fence. "No, there's nothing bittersweet about this."

"It's very sad," Jesse said, not ready for a casual conversation about the imminent sale of The Chateau, but he realized Daffy was only kneeling on the ground, pulling weeds and discarding wilted sunflowers into a bucket.

Jesse paced from the patio to the house and then back outside, eventually finding Mars looking over a mesmerizing triptych of Warhol silkscreens with which he'd long been familiar.

"Who is it?" she asked, about the model, and for good reason. Warhol had used several men while shooting the image, which revealed nothing more than adolescent peach thighs, a thin rub of hair around the navel, a healthy cock, coiled into Fruit of the Looms. Each was stamped "Andy Warhol—This photograph may not be etc." The figure retained the posture of Warhol's most commanding pieces—the bravado was in the indifference—and the multiplicity of the works themselves doubled down on the overindulged atmosphere of Jesse's downstairs area. "It's either Joe D'Allesandro or Paul America," he shrugged.

Bernie called to Jesse from upstairs. He and Cheryl were leaving, and Jesse, feeling an unexpected swell of emotion, followed his father to the front entranceway as they made promises of a regular phone call each week to begin re-entering each other's lives.

"How do you feel?" Lee asked, wiping down the counters, the two of them alone in the kitchen.

"I feel," Jesse broke off, "I'm doing okay." Then he found his manners. "So how do you feel?"

"Like myself, at least at this moment," Lee said. "I appreciate the company." He was spraying organic cleaner onto the counter, wiping it with brown recycled paper towels. "She's lovely," he said about Mars, "but you knew that."

"Yeah," Jesse said.

Upstairs Mars had begun running the bath in the large guest bathroom, initiating the whining start to the faucet, then the rush of noise through the plumbing. Lee smirked then quickly uncorked a nearby bottle of wine left over from dinner.

"Striking, really," he added, holding the wine up to the light, then bringing it beneath his nose, taking his time with it. "Is she much older?"

Jesse dragged his shoe across the kitchen tile, back and forth, burying his head. "She is," he exhaled after some time, bracing for vocalized statements of reason he'd been repressing all summer. But Lee went elsewhere.

Mars slept at The Chateau that night. When Uncle Lee had gone to bed they went out to the pool so their conversation wouldn't wake him. Mars changed into a one-piece zip swimsuit she'd packed for Palm Springs, which was dramatic and unnecessarily sexy in its current context. She lowered herself into the hot tub and began asking Jesse to bring her things: mineral water, a beer; later a towel. She showered as Jesse made his bed on the sofa; he packed her a bowl of OG Kush, a medical-grade bedtime strain she'd been recommended specifically for generalized anxiety disorder. It smelled like Lemon Pledge and tasted like earth and Pine-Sol. *Good job not drinking* resonated in Daffy's voice. He hadn't drank today, but he knew in Daffy's mind weed was the same: a substance that changed how he felt, thought or believed. It felt so good right now, and euphoria overpowered him as he lay on his bed, his eyes sealed shut.

Mars changed into a matching cotton pajama set—powder blue with white piping—then snuck around him as he slept, careful not to wake him as she slid into the bed, scooting next to him, Jesse still in his clothes, on top of the covers, and they slept until dawn, when Jesse stripped to his underwear and got under the sheets with her, his half-aware, languid attempts to fool around swatted away with equal lethargy, though once Mars was fully rested, she woke him up, eager now that it was her idea.

It would be something droll: their first fight.

They got up late. Lee and Daffy had gone on a hike. Jesse wanted to bring something to Mars' family's, where she was meeting everyone for the party, and he was feeling anxiety over it as he looked over the kitchen. He decided to make guacamole, the only appropriate dish he knew how to prepare, and leisurely chopped Serrano chili and halved limes, as Mars hovered. She threw in an extra pinch of cumin into the large molcajete as coffee brewed, overstepping a bit into Jesse's measured world, not that he'd said anything yet. When she tried to sneak a large scoop of mayonnaise into the mix he unapologetically scooted the bowl away, asking her to stand down. She acquiesced and pouted, explaining she'd learned the trick from her mom as a way to stretch portions. Jesse was surprised there was mayonnaise in The Chateau, knowing Lee, though when his back was turned again she snuck it in. When he caught on, he became petulant and snapped. He grabbed the jar and saw the expiration date had passed.

"Okay, sorry," she said, meaning it. "Well, here's some coffee, anyways."

Mars carried the guac as they passed through the one-story house into the backyard. Her youngest brother Justin was playing catch with their father. Both paused to greet Mars, then waved to Jesse without interest. He joined them, surprised himself by catching the football, passing in his best jock drag.

Mars' mother was sitting on a picnic table next to her sister Mable, who had a friend with her, both lost in their phones. They all soon began taking selfies with Mars. Mrs. Arenas, as she introduced herself, was drinking a tropical looking drink, and didn't offer to make one for anyone else as she sat next to the blender. She noticed the coals had gone white and called "Brauli," Mars' dad, over to put the meat on.

Mars told Jesse stories about her family on the way over. How her father was only interested in his own interiority. Her mother's children functioned to reflect her image back to her. "When she looks in your eyes, she's checking her lipstick in the reflection."

"My parents were very...corporeal," she said. "Once my dad grabbed my face in his hand so hard my jaw hurt for a week. Another time my mom took me by the hair and held me while she slapped me for having a smart mouth."

"You have to eat a few with the shells on," Brauli said to Jesse, reaching into a bag of peanuts that was near the grill. He handed a few to Jesse then popped one into his mouth and swallowed it after a few seconds. Jesse did the same, crunching down into the salty mess, though no one was watching. Mrs. Arenas was positioning Justin in various poses so she could post a birthday picture in his new sports jersey. Mars had pulled her sister aside and was giving her and her friend a secret present, and Jesse could hardly believe his eyes. They were Chanel bags, and he could faintly hear her explain they'd been gifts from Marc, which truly excited them, and she was re-gifting them as a breakup cleanse. He'd bought both, at a tag price near five-thousand each, when she couldn't decide if she wanted the calfskin accessory in white or navy blue.

❖

The family called him over to take photos, first alongside the awkward birthday boy, then with various combinations of the family. They set the camera on a timer and took a goofy group shot of everyone.

Jesse excused himself for the bathroom, and looked over their own wall of portraits from the family. There were so many siblings and relatives, which made deciphering the family tree a fool's errand. The house was small and very lived in— sneakers kicked off at the foot of the couch, plastic drinking cups here and there, candy wrappers.

Mars' dad came in and grabbed a beer from the fridge.

"How was Marsy's speech?" he asked, cracking the can and holding it to his neck and temple for cool relief.

"She's a professional," Jesse said.

"Vee, her mom and I, always worked on her speaking skills, I'm a great orator myself."

He grabbed a second beer and extended it out toward Jesse. When Jesse balked, Brauli nodded encouragingly.

"Doctor said I can't," he said, rubbing at his waist. The enthusiasm wilted from Brauli's face. "Bathroom?" Jesse asked, and Brauli told him the way.

Jesse slipped out front to the driveway and called Daffy, kicking at weeds at the edge of the lawn.

"Hey, Jesse, what's going on?"

"I think I might drink, I'm at a party..."

"Okay. Good job calling me first. What's going on?"

"Nothing you don't know, it's a family get-together, I don't know, people are having beer and frozen drinks."

"Think about the last time you drank, and what happens to you, generally, after you have that first drink," Daffy said, not knowing it was two nights before that this latest example had taken place. Jesse was quiet. "You can't safely drink, because you don't know what is going to happen to you and the people you're with. Jail, institutions, death...that's the kind of drinking we do."

Jesse saw Mars and her sister and friend smoking a joint away from the gathering. They didn't know he could see them.

"Yeah, some of the kids are smoking weed now. I want that, too."

"Get a can of soda, they won't push if you're holding something. Don't focus on the drinking. Just be kind, don't think about the beer, think about what you can contribute to the gathering. Remember, patience will always get you what you want."

"Yeah, okay, I feel better, thank you."

"Jesse."

"Yeah, I'm still here."

"I'm proud of you."

The guacamole had been well-received and was eaten entirely. Jesse threw the ball some more and felt a deep melancholy when the afternoon came to an end. He pleaded briefly with Mars to go with him back to The Chateau, but she wanted to stay with her family that night, and in the days before she went back to New York for good, and the whole family warmly and cheerfully sent him off.

Chapter 7: Today is the Last Day of Your Life

Jesse was given a space to live on the top floor of the same building where the haunted house was being constructed. He spent the end of July and August in regimented daily routine: he'd work from early morning until dusk, hanging out on-site of the house, documenting the progress online among the yells and knocks and prop adjustments and band-saws screaming through wood, spreading sawdust. He ate lunch with the team to eavesdrop on the morning's work, catching up with the directors and budget coordinator and team of interns. He was the youngest among them, and as they talked over the outline he'd presented on his first day, the project needing quick direction, the new form brought out the mutability of his narrative, and they deepened possibilities while adapting his script to a lived-in world. He gladly submitted to domination by the mechanism of the writing group, wishes of the investors, needs created by the intense competition of the Halloween market, with so few weekends to lure customers, and the season's other wicked seductions available to them at every turn. It was also a formative experience should he sell his script. They were happy days.

His work had ended when he turned in the storyboard, so he suggested he run their social media accounts, applying the lessons he'd learned from Mars about online branding to create hype about the haunted house. With the entire canon of horror films at his disposal, he posted moodboards and inspiration, shots around the work site, make-up tests, lots of goofing off with cast members.

In the evenings he was working on a crash rewrite of his television script. When he felt lonely he'd stalk Mars online, with whom he'd been devastatingly out of touch. He traced her travels through the trail she left online. He was otherwise alone.

New York City was its best at night, when it turned on all the lights; a sequined gown draped over a chorus of idle footsteps. The leisured observer was rarely rewarded during daytime, and he felt all public space here had been reduced to theater, where he could only look at other people or buy things.

He'd abandoned his own digital labor. Only one daytime talk show had contacted him about an appearance, and they'd stipulated he'd need Mars to be with him. When her agent responded that she had a conflict, they dropped him; interest in his victimization had pulled out like the tide. He was devastated when he applied the same reasoning to his relationship with Mars, that he'd become irrelevant to her. The heterosexual script of romance always offered a path to a happy ending.

On his first day off he went uninvited to Mars' loft apartment off the J train and rang her buzzer. She'd been in Hong Kong, then Tokyo, and after she'd posted a selfie in Budapest (he'd misrecognized it), Jesse believed she'd returned to New York. After some time, a male's voice cracked through the speaker and Jesse was let into the industrial building. When he got to the apartment the door was cracked open, which led him to a hallway that opened to an expansive living room-turned studio. A blonde girl he'd never seen before was filming herself doing yoga, topless in front of a computer. He stood looking away, then finally faked a cough to get her attention; when she asked "What the fuck?" he had nothing to say in response.

"I'm looking for Mars."

"Oh," she said, crossing her chest with her arm and standing up quickly. She disappeared into a back room, the threshold of which was only a curtain, and finally a short guy in a tank top, toned with freckled shoulders, came out from a back room reeking of pot and moving slowly as if he'd just woken up.

"Mars isn't here," he said. "I don't know where she is. Let's figure that out, my dude." He introduced himself as Ethan, squeezing down on Jesse's hand. The blonde girl came back out wearing a black sports bra, and when she got to her mat, she hesitated before restarting her routine. "Come on back," he said, drawing the curtain. The hall was lined with unpainted drywall board; half-open bedroom doors revealed raw beams lofting unmade beds. Light didn't reach much of this part of the apartment.

"It's like a haunted house back here," Jesse said.

"People, not places, are haunted, my dude," Ethan said. His room was at the back of the space—the door had no knob—and was inversely decorated to the spare rest of the raw loft, with its clutter of clean modern furniture and antique pieces from estate sales; a vase nurtured luxurious Monstera deliciosa fronds. The back of the room bloomed with a monstrous elephant-ear tree, its wide leaves obscuring the corners of the room with its cover and shadow. Opposite he had a view of the distant skyline from the large casement windows. The rest of the walls were dedicated to whiteboard—he'd drawn abstract charts all over them.

"Lay down, man," he said, pointing to a large leather sofa, pulling him out of a jealous reverie. "They're just things," he said, noticing Jesse's bewilderment. "So, how do you know Mars?" he asked.

"Old friend, or new one, rather," Jesse said.

"Mars and I used to hangout in Venice when we were just wee babes, teens, I guess," Ethan said. "She thought of me as her guru. I've always had this way of reading things." He pointed to the charts. "It's a Japanese candlestick method. Even I thought I had psychic powers. I was handling the market so well, now I just do it for myself and one or two clients. I made my first million when I was still in undergrad." He reached for a nearby ashtray, lifted from it a half-smoked joint.

"You're a millionaire?"

"Yeah, man." He lit it, inhaling performatively, then kicked off his flip flops and began a sun salutation, easing from an upward salute into a forward bend, joint still in hand. "I have to be careful with this, it's a strong sour diesel. It's my workday weed," he said, now in a high lunge, his left leg planted between his palms. "It's messy."

Jesse didn't know what to say, and impatiently recapitulated how he'd come to find himself in the situation.

"That's intense," Ethan said, touching his stomach in earnest empathy. "Want to hear a some fucked up shit, my dude?" He pushed up into plank.

"Not really."

"Do you know who Angelina Jolie is?" He went into downward facing dog, exhaling the words toward the floor.

"Everyone knows who she is, my dude," Jesse mocked him.

"My dude," Ethan cautioned, "relax." He slid his right foot forward, then eased into a forward bend, which he compromised by holding his arm out to Jesse, passing him the joint to ash.

Jesse set it in a ceramic ashtray, shaped as a caricature of Lucifer lying face-up—black eyes, black horns—the mouth hanging open and extended wide in a mocking howl, creating a pit to hold the ash. Jesse lifted it, and saw the stamp on the bottom.

"That's Bavarian. Expensive."

Jesse recognized the faint blue stamp on the bottom: Royal Bayreuth. A memory involuntarily came to mind, as he started feeling a contact high, of an artifact his mother and father had once owned from the same company, a ceramic tortoise that held creamer. He'd doted over it as a child for its vicious-looking face, its hollow neck and extended open mouth forming the spout. "Can you bring me a hit of that?" Jesse obliged, walking over and holding the joint to his mouth, letting him pull for a second or two before taking it away.

"What was I saying before all of this, oh, so I'm—this is secret, okay, my dude? I'm an angel investor in some experimental biopharmaceuticals. Do you know what Argireline is? And how peptides and amino acids work?"

"Um," Jesse said, not following, or sure he wanted to.

"So I got in on the ground floor on some next-level shit. I was jet skiing at Phuket, and I see this guy with his son, their jet ski is stalled, they're stranded. When I get close I realize it's Brad Pitt and one of his kids. And they're waving from this weird hidden lagoon area. So I trade them my jet ski, and wait on theirs while they head back. But on their way in they have an accident, and the kid hurts his leg or something. I'm not bullshitting, you can read this online, my dude." He eased into plank pose, talking as his toned muscles faintly tremored. "So they forgot all about me. I waited hours out there, getting sunburned. I start trying to get the jet ski running on my own, but it's a no-go, my dude. I turn the key and it just keeps clicking. Nothing. I'm trying to be zen but there is no love from the zen gods out there that day. So now I'm desperate and start shaking the thing like crazy, rocking it and panicking because the sun is starting to go down and I'm, like, surrounded by darkness and shit. I need a miracle, anything, I'm shouting. I crank it again and then the jet ski started! Turns out a fat-ass snake was caught in the intake pump. Once the fucker wiggled just a bit, I was back in action. I dragged him all the way back to the resort."

From plank, Ethan slid his legs towards his chest and stretched into child's pose. He held it for twenty seconds before moving into corpse pose, just breathing.

"So then what happened?" Jesse said, snapping to the present.

"My dude," Ethan said, grinning now that Jesse had expressed interest, "so the next day I get a note at my door—I'm staying at Amanpuri, do you know that place, bungalows and hammocks and villas and all of that?"

"No."

"Aw, man, go there, it's gorgeous. Anyway, Brad Pitt is staying at the same resort, in one of the villas, and he invites me for a scotch, as a thanks, and we get to talking. Next thing you know I'm changing funds into cryptocurrency, and transferring it to a total stranger. A cool two million. But I've always known what to say yes to. And you know who you don't say no to?"

"Tyler Durden?"

"Angelina Jolie. It's her initiative called Accellate," Ethan responded earnestly.

"Okay?"

"Yeah, so months go by after that, and the private team of scientists in Europe or wherever, who knows, get swaddled in delays over availability of materials, in-fighting, so this artificially intelligent organic 'smart cell' compound, Accellate, Angelina's dream, there's nothing to show for it after a year despite all of the capital we've invested. Correspondence is sparse, and always sent from encrypted accounts. Then suddenly we get an email, subject line 'damage control,' because Angelina and Brad's split has leaked to the media, and Accellate's cybersecurity was hacked. So the entire operation is about to implode, I hear from one side, then the other, but I happen to know a mastermind hacker, so I hire him to research the investment trails back to various international accounts, and it's no shocker who the players are once he gave me his list of names. Once I had that, I popped some popcorn and watched it blow up. The scientists mastered the technology, that was no problem. They'd conquered death, beat God, but the team wanted to bring it to the medical sector. Angelina stopped that, threats were made, the lab was raided; an inside job, right? But when Brad and Angelina couldn't resolve their trouble in paradise, the fighting escalated, and that's when Kris Jenner came in, and the war for ownership truly started. Most of these investors are global elite, people who would also live in space if they could, or cryogenically freeze themselves. They're chasing immortality, see what I'm saying, my dude? There was an enormous deposit linked to Suri Cruise's trust fund. That's a ten-year-old, by the way. But then one day, before it caught even a second of public attention, the melee stopped. A month later you get shot in a sloppy assassination attempt on Kim Kardashian's life. Then she gets robbed in Paris by masked men, investors coincidentally get an email saying research has been halted for good, the company is no longer raising funds, the technology has been lost. I received my two million back plus healthy interest, everything's rosy. But just this morning my friend, the hacker, traces the email server to an address on Greenport, out on Long Island. It seems we've been bought out, not divested. So I asked Mars to go check it out for me because I think she's out there. She's in Montauk for a wedding or a shoot or something, right, and Greenport is just a skip across the harbor. Problem is, she's not interested."

"Why not?"

"Because, what did she say, I'm a fucking 'rich, bored stoner,' her words, with a 'paranoid, time-wasting imagination,' also her words. I mean, what does it sound like to you, my dude? Says I need to get out of the hot box. That's what she calls this place."

Ethan excused himself to take a phone call. Jesse wafted through smoke from the powerful weed while stroking the thick, waxy ears of one of the plants he'd been admiring, realizing it was fake, and several grotesque faux Alocasias lay at its feet, with smaller plastic cacti and plastic succulents beside them.

He stared at a plastic fern, feeling stoned now, thinking of the odious phrase "plant butcher," a trend with a meaning that remained obscured, which he'd read in a magazine on one of his recent flights. He went back to the Monstera fronds on an end table near the sofa he'd been reclining on and touched them. He was glad to judge they were real, with small scabrous spots and hints of spider webs about the tucks of the curves. He pinched the biggest one of the fronds, thinking of its nickname, "Swiss cheese plant." He examined the underside, and found a black welt that turned out to be a real cockroach, which crawled up his fingers onto his hand. He wagged it off in a panic.

"Let's draw your chart, my dude," Ethan said when he came back. He was drinking something green out of a mason jar, now wearing a short sleeved button up, spread open over his chest. Jesse saw there was no getting out of it. "It's a system where

I build upper and lower shadows, real bodies, one instance at a time. I'm looking for movement and micro-narratives. I can explain it once it's all drawn. First we need a time frame we're working inside. Could be a week, month, year, five years."

"Let's do the past month."

"Okay, give it all to me like you did before, but don't leave anything out." Ethan drew the hieroglyphic rectangles as Jesse slowly explained everything to him, from the hospital on, talking for almost an hour.

"I remember driving with her over a bridge, looking out over the Pasadena Freeway, it's such a moving experience. Downtown looked like the Emerald City with the dry river running up to it," Jesse said, with his eyes closed. Ethan continued looking over the data he'd created, biting his lip as he zeroed in. Jesse delighted in the chance to share his stories, especially from this summer, though the strenuousness of their conversations had overpowered him, and he was nodding off.

"You're down, due for a correction, looks like, I'm giving you a hold rating, hold steady, sailor," Ethan said, from a place of deep focus, but all of it was meaningless, Jesse was asleep, and Ethan left him to rest.

He woke later when he felt a body sitting next to him, and when he opened his eyes, he saw Mars, smiling devilishly as she sank snug against his side on the edge of the sofa.

"Whether it's business or personal, your data is here to stay," she recited. "Carbonite cloud and hybrid data protection combines advanced backup, rapid recovery and anytime, anywhere access." He felt too drugged to respond; she was being incomprehensible. He felt the instinctual longing for the embrace that comes seconds after waking up next to someone.

Instead, she took him by the hand and led him out to the main room he'd passed through hours before. It was empty, no one was in the apartment. She walked ahead of him, a slower, sexier version of her long-perfected catwalk, cervine and controlled. She collapsed onto a couch, her dress spilling up over her waist. "Drop the pants," she ordered, lifting her leg onto the sofa. Jesse began taking off his belt as she lay splayed before him, rubbing her clit with one hand, working her fingers deep inside her vagina with the other. He watched her face contort and change as she moaned with pleasure, and when she opened her eyes she was pleased to see he was doing the same. She removed her hand from herself and ran her wet fingers over the rim of a wine glass on an end table, then held it out to him. "Come with me, Jesse, to a world of what, to you, remain unsealed pleasures."

Jesse woke hours later, deep into the night; it was four a.m. and he was in Ethan's room alone. Music reverberated from down the hall. His mouth felt stamped shut from dryness. He went looking for water.

He'd slept through most of the party that had been raging on the other side of the apartment. Scent-waves of latex and body heat rushed over him as he entered the space. Red light shone over bodies. Antagonistic music relentlessly blasted—the song was *Testure* by Skinny Puppy, but he didn't recognize it. A gothy twenty-something was playing YouTube videos on her laptop, to the approbation of the crowd, fueling everyone with darkwave and industrial ambience. Everyone looked like someone he sort of knew.

A guy slumped against the wall turned from semi-consciously kissing a girl on his right toward the mouth of the boy on his left, who exhaled smoke into his lungs as they then began making out. Some people were dancing, stripped just to lingerie. A couple was fucking missionary on the floor while several people watched, just standing there.

"Bunny baked a cake," a girl with long brown hair said to Jesse, as he neared her orbit. A random boy ran up behind her, wrapping her in his arms, his hands groping wherever. She giggled gleefully as they shuffled away.

"Who do you know here?" another girl asked. "I mean, who did you come here with?" She had on a leather slave collar and an open silk robe, revealing an empty strap-on harness. He told her Ethan, his mouth to her ear as he strained to talk over the music.

She opened a bag of coke and tipped some onto her fist, then held it out to him. "Go ahead," she nodded. "I'm good," he mouthed. She shrugged and snorted it herself, then stood there next to him taking in the scene alongside him.

Pleasure, he thought, letting his eyes go to the ceiling past the drugged crowd, the dark textured music and scattered scarlet neon and all of what this girl smelled like, she was standing so close to him, white jasmine and mint and basil, *it is so delicate and diaphanous.*

In the kitchen, Jesse gulped a coconut water he stole from the fridge. A second man came in, towering and wearing a rubber Frankenstein mask. He paused and stood before Jesse, who cowarded before the effect of the undead rubber eyes. Ethan appeared at the kitchen threshold, clothed, seemingly sober, holding a beer. He put a hand on Frankenstein's shoulder.

"My dude," Ethan said, interrupting the stand off. He stepped to Jesse and said, "Let me introduce you to someone who might be a little more age-appropriate for you," taking him to another room of the loft where a few people were hanging out, including the girl who'd offered him coke. She introduced herself as Lysette. They shared a joint while a British boy rambled about politics to a tan girl with a shaved head, who lay across his chest. TODAY IS THE LAST DAY OF YOUR LIFE, a postcard said, pinned to her wall. Jesse hadn't even seen it yet: it was an ad for his haunted house, giving away nothing but an address, and a date, white text on black gloss, and the title of the attraction Jesse had spent hours dwelling over. Jesse compressed the story about how he ended up back in New York City, his role with the haunted house, the absinthe, Palm Springs, all of it. They exchanged numbers and he promised her a priority walk-through before the haunted house opened.

The party was over, Lysette kicked everyone out of her room. Ethan stopped Jesse on his way out and handed him a book. "I've been revisiting this, but you should take it," he said. It had a soft cover, made of white matte linen, smudged a bit where thumbs rub when it's held, a minimal design with a simple, serif typeface: *Lullaby*, by Marsy-Rose Arenas.

Published when she was Jesse's age, Mars' interiority lay parceled in his hands like a fortune cookie, words so easily read, their meaning so undirected. The poet was someone he knew and didn't know: young, brash, powerful and sexy. He had taken a picture of the cover and was seconds from sending it to Mars, then he thought better of it.

Sunrise contended with street lamps as he rode the subway back into the city. He felt unaccountably hungry and exited at Delancey-Essex, then walked through the Lower East Side into the East Village, where only the most and least enfranchised were on the streets. He ended up at a deli with a steaming cup of coffee, reading his new book over a smoked salmon and cream cheese bagel, capers toppling into his lap.

Negligé

Owning the manor
In a nightie
Smoking cigarettes
In the Hollywood wind

A piece of paper fell out of the pages. It was a torn page with the messy handwriting Jesse recognized as Ethan's from the whiteboards. It contained an address and nothing else. He typed it into Google maps and it brought up a location in Greenport. Jesse stuffed the paper back in the book and headed back home.

A box was waiting on his doorstep. Bernie and Cher had sent him a care package; in it was a blank DVD with *Until I See Palm Trees Again* written on it. On a sunny autumn morning, big blue sky over the waking city, Jesse sat down and pressed play.

The intro theme was a complicated flight of woodwinds, brass and strings, threatening to dip into a minor key, lovely and elegiac. The first image was a fixed camera angle from the foot of a long driveway facing a house. In the first few seconds, a time lapse starting in the dark of the a.m. sped to daybreak, daybreak rushing to blues of noon, abstract car or two in and out of the driveway, a package delivery, the mailman.

Jesse had studied the cast list many times in his life. Familiar names of actors and actresses appeared over clips from the show; it was the faces Jesse didn't recognize, their movements and theatrical gestures adding up to a string of fragments from a world that was and wasn't his. Cut to the time lapse: house at dusk, lights coming on in the windows, movement in the gold-lit rooms, the gables and impressive spire of the Victorian-revival home, moonrise, a crescendo, starlight beyond. It was nothing like Jesse's actual, more modest, one-story Craftsman structure he'd grown up in in West Adams.

The scene opened with "Jesse" driving with his dad, who was taking a call, on what must have been a fourth or fifth driving lesson. They were in the hills, and the actor playing Jesse was more hawkish and handsome than he should have been. Bernie's portrayer was more accurate with his sweater over an oxford, the casual professional dad's uniform, better complexion, thicker hair, thinner body. He talked on the phone as Jesse drove through the hills, being cautious, both hands on the wheel, nervous, and as a car came around a bend, Jesse drifted just a bit off the road and the tire blew.

"Easy now," Bernie said to calm him. "Gonna have to call you back!" he shouted into the phone. Cut to the actors looking at the blown tire. Two cars racing, one behind the other, burn past them. Bernie frowns and begins dialing.

Establishing shot of the house: dull olive paint, faded mustard trim, dwarf palmetto palm, and a budget Linda Evans, the actress playing his mother, painting the door an indulgent pale pink. The old-sounding ring of a landline played and the scene cut to inside the house. They'd wasted no time getting to the conflict and establishing the dilemma. In the one-sided conversation to Jesse's father: "So you didn't tell him," following with, "No, you're right, I guess it wouldn't have been appropriate. No, we're heating up leftovers. Okay, love you."

Jesse watched his past in standard definition as he sat unprotected against what he imagined awaited, but as the next scene began, the DVD froze. Jesse paused stoically before the glitching miasma on the screen. He played a tug-of-war with it, rewinding and fast-forwarding, then finally ejected the DVD and gave it a careful cleaning. He played it again, watching the same opening scenes, but the disc would proceed no further. He stood up angry and went to the window, staring past the pompous midtown skyline, dissociating. His phone rang. It was a producer from the haunted house—he'd forgotten he promised to drive up with him to Long Island for the day and visit another haunted Halloween attraction, one they were bundling tickets with in a cross-promotion, and there was no getting out of it. The producer was sick from food poisoning and begged Jesse to go instead.

Jesse had grown accustomed to the easy loneliness of traveling. He floated with minimal effort as the Prius practically drove itself. He typed the destination on his phone and gave himself to his thoughts, wherever they went, as he was directed onto the expressway. Outside the car, the air cooled to an emotional pitch. Summer was over; he felt it on the windows, and he thought of the representation of his home as he'd seen it on his mother's show, the colors seemingly unlike her, the gesture of it more so, and he realized now the concurrent timelines his mother had deployed, how in the first scene his father had not been calling his mother at all since she'd already passed away, but instead perhaps a new lover, or a relative—he couldn't know—and the coincidence of the phone calls with the abrupt cut to mom painting the door while the phone rang: it was a red herring. And the door! That must be the heart of the whole series; a play on color, the rotting green and yellow of the house giving way to the optimistic, ironized gesture of the pink door. And for Patricia to write a scene where Bernie would have taught him to drive, when it was Uncle Lee who had done so in real life: he felt crushed by his failure to live up to the optimism she'd projected onto a future she knew she wouldn't live in.

Jesse checked his phone, the directions were paused. He'd been driving the wrong way for quite some time. The GPS dot still placed him somewhere on Long Island. He took an exit and stopped to buy a sugar-free Red Bull. Scrolling through his apps, he felt goosebumps at a new picture of Mars in his feed. She was curled like a cat, deep in the comfort of an outdoor sofa, party lights strung and rippling water beyond. She had on leggings and an oversized sweater, her hand held up her chin as she grinned at a lucky someone out of the frame. The geotag on the post placed her at a hotel and resort: *Chilly days, cool nights. Filming beach scenes this week.* He looked up the most expensive resort in the area and decided it was worth half a try.

The cloud cover that rolled in offered little romanticism to the mission he imagined himself to be on, and the desperate truth of the absurd decision to visit began asserting itself: he was acting out.

At Sunset Beach, he had to park far and walk a good distance to finally merge among the overcrowded outdoor bars, stuffed with weekenders scraping against the newly monied as they live-action-role-played life as those with old money. Striped awnings gestured a South of France mise-en-scene as the sun crashed red beneath the thinning distant cumulonimbus clouds. Jesse didn't see Mars anywhere on the grounds. He left with his head hanging, wondering what he looked like to those peering out among the revelry, but conceived himself only as a vague outline, a background character.

Making a blind turn near the ferry exit, an Escalade passed too close and clipped his side view mirror, and when the driver stopped, Jesse leered hard through the SUV's thick tinted windows, seeing only a bald, thick-necked driver with sunglasses on, though when the passenger window rolled down, and a child's arm dropped a piece of trash, Jesse saw a familiar woman's face appear through the opening in the graying light of dusk. It was Angelina Jolie! The Escalade sped off as Jesse made a three point U-turn, his heart racing.

They were separated at a red light. Jesse kept them in his distant sight, speeding to catch up, zooming in with his phone to take a picture of the car and license plate, not sure why he was willing to break every law. He'd plead with her for a few moments' time, to explain about Lee's condition and how he could benefit from a product such as Accellate.

The Escalade turned onto a dirt road. It was unclear if they were aware Jesse was following. He was deeper in the country now. He looked at the map on his phone, having to zoom out to get his coordinates in relation to the landmarks he recognized. Cell service was limited. No one knew where he was. He was far from the crowded ferry to Shelter Island, and Sag Harbor, that tediously charmed hamlet, or beyond, the most TV-ready destination: The Hamptons, that locked kingdom of boutiques and restaurants, high-hedges and legacy homes with their private coves and beaches.

Just seeing its name reminded Jesse of scrolling through television channels, or a magazine. At another red light the Escalade pulled away from him for good. Jesse reached into his backpack, panicking, and typed the address from the scrap of paper in his phone; it didn't exist, and Google recommended a nearby location instead. He was alone on the road. As he drove, he passed a golf course, then dense woods—he imagined them crawling with diseased ticks for miles.

Spotlights shone over the dirt and gravel. The lot the pin on his phone sent him to had a large brick structure with an exterior in disrepair. Tall chain link fences bordered the property, giving way to the dark forest around. Two small white Ford trucks with government plates were parked in a muddy lot, side by side, hundreds of feet beyond the entrance. The security booth was empty and the electronic gate was jammed open. His eyes traced a set of new looking tire tracks around the side of the building, beyond where he could see.

It was cold and he was underdressed as he approached the property. He'd abandoned the citizen-in-need story when he slowly lifted the gate, which squeaked violently. He kept quiet as he crept to the side of the lot, out of the light, against the fence, the wind pulling through the trees. The scene from *Blow Up* of David Hemmings lurking in the park came to mind, though wasn't that actor wearing bright white chinos? Jesse dropped the noir psychoscape and walked to the side of the building. There was no sign of the Escalade, though a black hole the shape of a door was cut out of the brick wall near a loading dock; a camera mounted above seemed to be pointing right at him, but the case was shattered and it was empty inside—a decoy. Jesse turned the flashlight on his phone and began talking himself into entering the complex when he got a text:

Hey babe, what are you doing on LI?

...

Here for work. I don't have plans after, are you free, by any chance

Wrap party! You should crash it

Oh, ok! Where?

Surf lodge, already started so come whenever

Kk

Muah!

"Dude, what'd I say? Don't park out front." A man was stepping down from a loading area at the back of the building. "You're early. Jake ain't even here yet. And kill the fuckin' light!"

Jesse tore off, ducking the gate. With the key in his pocket the doors unlocked automatically. He pressed the power button on the dash and yanked it into drive, smashing the accelerator as the automatic headlamps burst on. A tall figure in a denim jacket remained just beyond the gate, his arms in the air, gesturing "what the fuck?" into the night.

He laughed it off once he was back in the car, a mile or two away, but something fleshy ran out into the path of his headlights, and he slammed the breaks. It was a girl in an oversized t-shirt, naked from the waist down—peroxide blonde with pitch-black roots—screaming for help, shivering, blood in her hair and on her arms and thighs. He had been on a long service road and could see the lights of a gas station and a 7-Eleven ahead.

"You have to help me, just get me out of here!" She was crying. Mascara ran down her face.

"This is fucking crazy!" Jesse yelled, choking the wheel, his mind a whir of split-second thoughts. He opened the door and she jumped in.

"Oh my god, you saved my life," she gasped. "There's a phone booth a half a mile away, I can call 911," she said, choking for air. He sped off again as she sobbed beside him. They reached the parking lot within seconds. "Don't leave me, please?" She jumped out and ran into the booth and dialed 9-1-1, or so it looked. Jesse rolled the window down to listen to her conversation as he scanned his surroundings. There was a car pulling out of the lot, and no one else was around except the attendant in the store, a middle-aged woman who was lost in a magazine at the register. Then Jesse noticed a black car near the dumpster at the opposite end of the parking lot. An open window was being used to steady a large camera from inside the car. The glass lens was pointed right at him.

"So, hey," the girl said, "I need another really big favor."

"What? Why?"

A man with a huge grin got out of the Escalade, clutching a clipboard while waving one arm in the air, bellowing "Aw, yeah!" and wolf-whistling while another person outfitted with a steadicam was zooming on Jesse's reaction.

"Is that that fucking reality-TV-producer-dickhead Sean Kennedy? You've got to be kidding me."

"Oh my god, you know him? That's my field producer! Sean, you are soooo popular!"

"Hey man, pat yourself on the back," Sean started celebrating. "You've totally proved you're a bona-fide good samaritan in front of our audience of tens of thousands."

"Omigod, if you don't sign this consent form my director will literally have kittens."

Jesse saw the girl had a GoPro strapped onto her thigh that had been filming his reaction to her initial plea for help and the car ride. "You've got to be fucking kidding me," he yelled in disbelief.

"Oh, no—babe, don't freak out, it's dry blood, it didn't get anywhere."

He gunned the car murderously at Sean, who was about fifteen yards away, and had to dive: papers flew around as the Prius chirped the tires.

The party at Surf Lodge was peaking. He parked among a flurry of Uber drivers waiting to pick up clients. A girl who looked like Cara Delevingne stumbled past with a Gigi Hadid clone. Actually, it was them. Zayn Malik ran by, rushing to the window of each of the similar-looking vehicles, interrogating drivers one by one: "Picking up Zayn? Zayn? Um, do I look like a 'Monica' to you?"

Card tables had been lined up as a makeshift security check upon entrance to the compound but were now abandoned by staff, and Jesse easily walked in and began looking for Mars. The movie's final scene had been filmed in Montauk. Liam Hemsworth called in a lifetime of favors to throw Jennifer Lawrence a sizzling star-studded soirée. Surf Lodge had been rented out for cast and crew and shuttles ran a sizeable overflow of extras and A-listers brought in for cameos to their neighboring hotels. A loud rock song was playing and several fire pits roared. Zach Efron walked by with Chloë Grace Moretz. Finally, he found Mars. She was holding the leash of an over-active doberman while a guy in a white t-shirt with short brown hair held up a key to her nose. She inhaled aggressively, did a hair flip, then saw Jesse.

"Jesse!" she yelled, a bit too loudly. "Oh my god. Jesse Shore. Jesse fucking Shore!" She stood up and stumbled towards him.

"Your friend is tits-wasted," a friendly voice said. It was Robin from Palm Springs. Adrian, too, appeared, frolicking up.

"Marsy-Rose Arenas, what's your secret?" Adrian pleaded, pretending to hold a microphone to her mouth.

"Ask doggy," she said, trying to get the dog to pay attention, who tugged away from her, over and over. Half-ventriloquizing in a puppy voice, she sang, "Dry shampoo, and lots of cuddles." She then turned to Jesse. He made the kissing noises he knew dogs loved, and immediately won the attention of the pup.

"Look at you," Mars said. "All you fucking do is touch lives." Then she began poking him on the shoulder. "Jesse Shore, Jesse fucking Shore. This guy is a genius," she said to Adrian and Robin, still poking at Jesse a little too hard. "No, seriously, he's a genius, just wait. He's creating this show. I bet you're writing a part for me, aren't you?"

Jesse and Adrian laughed as they watched Jesse try to find himself in the scene she was making. "Oh my god, where's Haley Bennett? Do you want to do coke with Haley Bennett?" She was slurring as she reached for a long-melted, long-abandoned margarita in a plastic cup. The doberman was darting away from Mars again, struggling to be freed.

"Hey, what the fuck," someone else said, walking up to them. It was Kendall Jenner. "That's my fucking dog!"

"Oh, but he's so sweeeeet," Mars said in a puppy voice.

Security promptly approached and asked Mars to leave; she began arguing. The scene turned aggravated. Jesse felt embarrassed for her, though when Jesse said they were together, they said it was fine if Mars just handed over the dog. Kendall approached Mars, who refused to release the leash. When Kendall stepped to grab it from Mars, Mars shoved her, both of them toppling into the sand.

"You fucking crackhead!" Kendall yelled as she tried to get up. "This is all your fault!" Mars yelled back. "Fucking sycophants!" Then Mars was escorted out, screaming at everyone, including the guards who had her by the arms, continuing to mutter pithy comments under her breath once they were at the property edge, where they stood watch to keep her from coming back.

In the parking lot she made a call, but whoever she was trying to reach didn't pick up, and she quietly began crying. "All my people are in there. I fucked up everything. Fuck." Jesse tried consoling her, explaining that people are forgiving, that everyone was drinking and that none of it would matter in a week.

"You're, like, a little *doe*, Jesse," Mars said, the words sounding thick on her tongue, her tone turning to disgust. "Do you even know who Sidney Kimmel is? You know, the film financier? He saw all of that. I'm so fucked."

"Hey, come on," Jesse said, but she brushed him away. He saw she was crying, makeup gobbing as her tears shone in the streetlights. A cab honked, and she jumped in.

Chapter 8: If I Close My Eyes

July and August blurred into the past, summer peaked, and the first chills of autumn touched the air. Jesse busied himself with work ahead of the opening on Labor Day weekend. He'd arranged his personal work area in the image of a television writer's room, with various whiteboards outlining the sections of the attraction. He'd stayed off drugs all fall; it had been a productive few months for him.

Things cooled between him and Mars since they'd last been together in Montauk. He wasn't hurt to have been the target of her ire, but instead accepted the more melancholy truth that their companionship wasn't serious, that even having met her was the illogical product of chaos; the good occasions they'd had belied the more than ten years between them and what they prohibited. The trajectory of their lives had crossed temporarily through the garden of forking paths, and fantasy, being that, is not supposed to actually be.

Investors had applied for a liquor license to run a pop-up bar next to the haunted house as an extension of the attraction. Jesse imported the redlighted orgy-ambience, decorating with leftover materials and supplies to offer a lush landing spot for adrenaline-fueled guests who'd just gone through the haunted house. Lysette was brought on as a principal bartender—everyone agreed she had the look—and it became common for the staff to end a long day's work behind the locked doors of the bar, screening horror films from a projector for inspiration while they drank and talked over it. Jesse'd even suggested an absinthe cocktail for the menu as a nod to Marilyn.

Nervous energy gripped him as he woke Friday morning on opening day. As he opened his eyes, he mused on the details of the dried milk thistle stalk Lysette had tattooed on her side, usually hidden by her arm. She'd made tea and returned to the unfolded futon, sipping sencha while reading news on her phone, the blanket peeled down to her waist. Autumn wind wrapped the block and streamed into the cracked windows of the Lower East Side building. Jesse rolled over, burying his face into her neck and hair, taking in her scent. They began kissing, then she slid on top of him and straddled his waist.

Lysette was an only child, like Jesse. Her father had died when she was young. She was raised by her mother, who she described as "more of a 'hippie' than an 'anarchist,' but kind of both, which was sort of hilarious, but also sort of tragic." When she channeled her mother's folk wisdom, which usually happened when they were discussing trauma, she did so as if speaking in quotations. Jesse's anxiety was constant since he'd be back in New York. Crowds, closed spaces, tunnels, startling noises and shouting were all threatening environments in which he felt little control. Lysette reminded him he was slowly renormalizing to his environment. "Listen to your body," she'd say, with a slight grin, when she saw him becoming tense. His body wanted sex and mammalian comforts, to be rubbed and touched.

Jesse stayed in bed after Lysette went down to receive some last-minute deliveries for the bar. He idly scrolled through his phone, half-noticing an image Mars had posted that seemed to break from the auto-pilot her accounts had been on. It was a picture of a pug, with the caption "What do you name something so tiny, harmless, naughty and cute? Thanks Kendall!"

"Kendall's Contretemp!" one of the more incendiary gossip websites posted when they ran a story about Mars' Montauk meltdown, accompanied by blurry photographs showing Kendall Jenner on the ground. More sympathetic coverage cast Mars as the victim of an unfortunate couple of months, having survived a psychotic gunman but also a public breakup, both in one summer.

Kendall publicly forgave her, and Mars was invited onto *Keeping Up with the Kardashians* to film a segment of the two shopping for puppies in the West Village, then having dinner together in Tribeca. Jesse scrolled through her feed and "liked" several posts for the first time in weeks. Moments later, Mars was inviting him to meet up in Central Park that afternoon.

Mars had on a white tunic and oversized sunglasses and her dog ran at her feet, under the wrought-iron table, tangling itself on its leash as she set her phone next to her maple latte. He'd met her at an ornamental pond inspired by the model boat ponds in Paris. Jesse talked excitedly about the haunted house, opening the bar, treading lightly around the fallout from the last time they saw each other when he updated her on Lee's positive well-being and the state of things back home in Los Angeles.

They walked and talked and Jesse felt the familiar and melancholy radiance in his chest that he always had to repress around her. Mars carried the dog for blocks while she told Jesse about auditions she had coming up this fall, the shows she had appeared on and what her encounters with the cast had been, though suddenly she paused. They were at 555 Fifth Avenue, inadvertently in front of the bookstore where the shooting occurred.

The exterior was dirty, and the window display had been reverted back to a slosh of the summer's familiar-looking best-sellers.

"Did we walk this way on purpose?" Mars asked.

"No," Jesse said.

"It's kind of anticlimactic, right?" Mars sighed. Then someone interrupted her.

"Oh my god!" the younger girl said, seeing Jesse and Mars. She was with a flock of peers in school uniforms, carrying the annoying energy of young teenagers turned loose after school.

Jesse braced to watch Mars take selfies or endure taunts or deflect questions about Marc, which had happened before.

"He's sooo cute! Can I pet him?" Mars gave Jesse a relieved look and set the dog down, who stood up with his tiny paws onto the girl's legs as her friends took videos on their phones.

"What's his name? How old is he?"

"Maybe I'll call him Jesse," Mars said.

"Jesse, you are too cute," the schoolgirl said, leaving them alone again, at last.

"You know what I really love doing?" Mars said. "Sharing a half-bottle of wine at The Plaza food court."

"I don't really drink, remember, and I'm not twenty-one, but I can see the appeal," Jesse said. He couldn't believe she'd forgotten something so central to his life.

"Right," Mars said. "How old are you again?"

"Nineteen?"

"Right." She sounded surprised. "Are you having a thing with that girl, the really cute one I've seen in your pictures?"

"I don't know," Jesse's head swirled. "It's um…"

"Oh my god, you're actually blushing," Mars said. "I'm so glad you never did that whole *I'm too stoic to care* thing guys do."

"Yeah, I guess I wouldn't know how?"

"And here I am, talking to my therapist on the phone all morning about if it's safe for me to fall in love with the person I've been seeing."

The immeasurable rush Jesse received in his split-second of wondering if this person could have been him passed to the obvious and crushing truth that it wasn't.

"What'd your therapist say?" Jesse could barely ask.

"Oh, who knows," Mars said, failing to coax the puppy into walking. Jesse's phone rang. It was one of his staff saying a *New York Times* journalist named Savannah wanted to talk to him about a piece she was writing about immersive therapy.

"I gave her that idea," Mars said. "While you were asleep in the back seat."

"Oh, thanks," Jesse said, still feeling sacked by the revelation that she had a new lover. A CitySights NY crawled by—the seats were mostly empty—and Jesse made eye contact with the guide, who was corralling the tourists' attention their way.

"Fuck this."

"Seriously."

"And it's the Ritz Tower!" the guide boasted. "Home of innumerable high profile New Yorkers and foreign buyers alike, including Clive Davis, and even former United States President Bill Clinton."

"People pay for that?" Mars rolled her eyes.

"Anyways, I should go. Do you want to come with me and see the house?"

"I can't right now, I'm sort of waiting for my—whatever he is, my boyfriend—to get to JFK. He's taking me upstate to his house for a romantic getaway or something. The whole long weekend thing. You know how these actor-boys are."

"Oh. Right," Jesse said, holding the swell of a sentence in, maybe the question of which actor, though probably not that at all. Either way Mars noticed, and they had an awkward pause in their conversation, as whatever Jesse was going to say remained caught in his throat.

"I've hurt a lot of people, Jesse…" Mars finally said.

"Yeah."

Haunted House Profits by Going Hollywood

By <u>Savannah Williams</u>

I'm seeing someone being murdered, but since I'm all alone I don't scream; I've been told no one will care.

After waiting around the block, and before entering the first chamber, I am sent into a security booth where a very large, shirtless guard lies slumped unconscious: belt a bit undone, sock stuffed in mouth.

Split-screen surveillance monitors show simultaneous shots of what seems to be happening ahead of me: unfocused shouting, bodies on the ground. Another younger male visitor seems to be crying and praying for his life.

The transmission fades and a new broadcast begins, the vague outline of a figure through static is talking to me: *Don't worry about him, he's dead! But listen to me and you'll be just fine...*

I'm then given the two rules of the house: forward is the only way out. Use my light-up "safe whistle" if things get too intense.

Today is the Last Day of Your Life is the newest addition to New York City's interactive theater offerings. It's not your parents' haunted house, or your children's either. No one under 18 is allowed into this indelicate hellscape.

The point is clearly not to give your nerves a safe tickle; it's to instigate and mess with your psyche. And it does this well.

Conceptualized with producer and shock-artist Marilyn Manson, the project was helmed by 19-year-old Jesse Shore, an aspiring screenwriter from Los Angeles who has yet to land his first pilot.

Jesse made headlines when he was errantly shot during a haywire attempt on Kim Kardashian's life that took place here in Midtown. He says working on the house has allowed him to work out some of his trauma.

For instance, after the initial vignette ends, visitors stumble through a long foggy tunnel that ascends the perimeter of the building (the ambient and mind-altering two minute walk feels like twenty). When the fog clears, you find yourself, of all places, at a shopping mall food court.

A breaking news cast loops on several flatscreens mounted high in the corner of the staged dining area. A woman eats alone. I hear heavy stomping, guns cocking, and I hear her screaming, instructing me to get down under one of the booths (I did!). I lie in fear as the shooter's steps approach, then retract, approach, then retract.

She held eye contact with me until the noise ended. The actress broke for the double doors (was the enormous EXIT sign lit up before?). The sound effects ceased as I found the nerve to dash out of the room as she did.

Today is the Last Day of Your Life offers lush horror and well-made Hollywood sets to deliver its fright (a Golden Globes-cum-funeral sequence is particularly clever). But its greatest aesthetic effect is that most of the action takes place inside your head.

Telling too much would spoil the thrill, but imagine a tense or nervous pause dragging on for minutes, drawn out into terror, but instead of enjoying it from the distance of your sofa, you're co-producing it.

Chapter 9: Epilogue

Jesse was watching television. It was his birthday, the solstice, and he'd come to Los Angeles to dither among succulents, get a base coat for a summer tan and see family. He was back in The Chateau—it hadn't sold—lying on the cool leather sofa, texting his father, who was in town for meetings. Jesse was trying to set up a few of his own.

After Halloween, when the haunted house and bar closed, Jesse went back to working at the denim boutique while finishing the script of his pilot, which he was able to get into the hands of a producer Mars recommended. She'd acted in the pilot for free, his father pulled some strings, and the show was picked up by CBS for a full season. Jesse was paid a few thousand dollars for his intellectual property rights and asked to sign a contract that gave him a writing credit, but otherwise took him off the project. *Paid to go away*, Cheryl had put it. He begrudgingly accepted the deal, on his father's advice, which was fine, until Lee let it slip that not only was Bernie being considered for executive story editor, but the studio was doing a table read with the topliners later that morning. Jesse felt he was at least owed a staff writer position. He got in his rental and charged toward Studio City.

His plan was to pretend to be his father, faking he'd lost his wallet, but otherwise he knew the right names to get him in the gate. Once inside, he'd talk his way into the meeting. His father would be too embarrassed not to let him sit in. He'd walk the halls to the conference rooms, he'd see Judd Apatow talking excitedly with his father, in a meeting with the writers, and when he approached the door, he'd be stopped by a young assistant, sitting behind a desk, phone in hand, ready to call security. Judd would see him and take pity on him, reluctantly letting him join. When he was introduced as the creator, the attendees would take interest, and Jesse could then begin beaming over his wealth of ideas for the different character's plotlines, one by one.

But this was only in his head.

As Jesse approached the gates, a motorcyclist who was leaving the studio pulled out in front of an approaching vehicle, and as the biker swerved and accelerated out of the way, the driver went over the handlebars and lay still on the street in a single-rider accident. Panicked citizens rushed to him from their cars.

When Jesse pulled to the gate, the second-in-command was playing no-nonsense, so when he feigned being Bernie Shore's assistant, he didn't get anywhere.

"He's had a family emergency," Jesse pleaded. "He isn't answering phones. His wife's condition has taken a horrible turn for the worse and doctors have requested him at the hospital immediately."

He was led to the conference room where the table read was taking place, but when he scanned the staff, his father wasn't among them, and he didn't recognize anyone in the room. This team was mostly guys in their thirties, and a few men in suits. A dog was walking down the table, sniffing water bottles. Jesse saw his show's name written on the wall and charged inside, violently banging on the glass door, scaring everyone. A security guard immediately showed up, followed by another. Jesse showed his visitor's pass, but they took him by the arm and walked him to the back elevators where no clients could see them escorting him out.

"Are you gonna be chill or what?" they said. "We call the cops on people because of this."

"Yeah, I'm chill," he said softly.

When he was walking back to his car someone called his name. It was Mars, being driven in a golf cart.

"I'm about to do the table read!"

A bored looking intern idled as Jesse approached.

"That's amazing," Jesse said.

"Yeah, I guess I got my break," she said, squinting at the sun behind him while making a visor with her hand. "The money guys want to check the chemistry between the principals and make notes on..." She trailed off, it wasn't Jesse's business. "Script problems, I guess." She had nervous energy and was effervescent in a way he'd never seen.

"How's life? Are you still with that guy, you know, the one you told me about the last time I saw you, ages ago?"

"Haha. Which one? But no. Wait, did you hear *Keeping Up with the Kardashians* finally got canceled?"

"No?"

"What are you doing here anyway? Did you just turn in an amazing new spec?"

"Yes, exactly that." He laughed.

"Well, you don't look LA-happy, but you look New York-good," she said. "That means life's been good to you. You and—what's her name—still going strong?"

"She dumped me a few months ago. She moved to Florida."

"I want to hear all about her one day," she said.

A walkie-talkie squelched from the intern's belt.

Hours later he floated in The Chateau pool, carefully holding his phone between his eyes and the late afternoon sun. He'd admonished Lee for being dead wrong about his father's involvement with the show, though when he confessed what he'd done, Lee simply responded, "You're kidding, right?" Jesse decided to lie: "I am."

He was receiving birthday messages from friends in New York, invitations to go out, but he was keeping his plans open to spend time with his family that night. Then he got a text from Mars.

Jesse! I was so caught up in my nervousness today
I forgot to say "happy birthday"

Haha. It's ok. I hope it went well.

It went great!
I'm just so busy with everything going on right now.
So sorry again!
Xo.

Jesse let it end there. He switched phone applications and saw Mars had just posted a photo from a year ago on this date, a throwback to what she called "the day that changed everything."

It was the same image he'd first seen of her when he searched for her name online, her open-mouthed, fixed glare into the camera. It was an image he'd long forgotten about, but one he'd been so fixated on in those first weeks after he'd met her. Had she known he'd saved it on his phone? He closed his eyes and gave the screen a kiss, a tender and senseless blur of breath from his nose and lips. Maybe he could change his flight and stay a little longer. Maybe he was already here and would stay.

Acknowledgments

Thank you to Francesca Kritikos and Will Carey at SARKA for seeing this manuscript through to publication.

An excerpt from this manuscript was published in *Joyland*, thanks to Kyle Lucia Wu.

Descriptions of television shows and films on pages 11-12 were sourced from various online outlets. Some have been altered for clarity.

Milton Keynes UK
Ingram Content Group UK Ltd.
UKHW040703151023
430644UK00002B/24